This is David Speaking

(formerly Truth or Dare)

Stephanie Ward

SCRIPTURE UNION
130 City Road, London EC1V 2NJ

First published 1975
Re-issued as THIS IS DAVID SPEAKING 1978
Reprinted 1978, 1981, 1984

ISBN 0 85421 598 0

Photoset in Malta by St Paul's Press Limited
Printed and bound in Great Britain by
William Clowes Limited, Beccles and London

Chapter One

'Mum, where's my dinner money?'

'Oh, I don't think I've got change today, love. Tell Miss Lawson I'll send it along tomorrow.'

'Yes, Mum!'

'That's funny,' thought David, 'I don't remember her forgetting it before. Mum's usually so particular about things like that, but then she does seem a bit vague this morning.'

David picked up his school bag from the table. It had 'Arsenal' written on it, and a picture of a footballer stamped in white. He didn't need a bag for school, but he liked to take one. Sometimes he carried his training shoes in it, or a football magazine. Today he had some football cards because there was a craze for playing 'flicks' in the lunch hours at the moment. He also had a couple of odd batteries and some wire for a model he was making.

'Bye then, Mum.'

'Bye love.'

David went out into the hall and quietly closed the door. Maybe his mum wasn't feeling too well this morning. She came to see him off as a rule.

He opened the hall cupboard and got out his training shoes. He wasn't allowed to wear them to school because his mum thought that they didn't give enough support for his feet. So he had to wear black lace up shoes, not even fashionable ones. This morning he didn't think she'd notice. His training shoes were blue and white. They were the best you could get and his dad had bought them for him. David didn't see much of his dad because he was a sales representative for a paper firm and he had to travel around a good deal. Sometimes he was away for a whole week.

David had just laced up his shoes when Alison came downstairs.

'Mum'll give you what for if she catches you in those.'

'She said I could wear them.'

'I bet! I'll go and ask her.'

'If you do, I'll tell her you wore eye shadow to school last week, so there.'

Alison laughed and thumped him as she went past into the back room.

'Bye, Davie.'

'Bye.'

Alison wasn't too bad as sisters went. She was thirteen and at the big comprehensive school up the road from David's. Sometimes David thought she was a bit bossy, and occasionally she cried and made a fuss about nothing, but usually she was all right. She was better than Sheila Jones next door anyhow. Sheila was awful, always hanging round with boys and cheeking her mum.

David opened the front door. The front garden was very small – his mum called it her pocket handkerchief. One stride from the front step and you were on the pavement, but it was still a garden.

He picked up Debbie's bike which had fallen into some plants. She often left it at the front propped up against the window. Their mum didn't allow them to take bikes and things through the house to the back and the only other way was up to the end of the terrace and along the alley. Debbie wouldn't go on her own because of the alsatian at number seven. So David had to go with her and if he wasn't there her bike stayed out all night.

'Don't blame me if it gets pinched, Debbie,' their mum often used to say. David didn't think anyone would take it, it was much too rusty.

Debbie had already left for school. She was eight, and two years younger than David. She had a student in her class this term and went early to help her carry her things.

David stepped out on to the pavement and looked to see if any of his friends were coming. They weren't so he began to walk towards school.

David lived on quite a busy road. It wasn't exactly a main road, but it was on a bus route, and there were shops on it. None of the houses at David's end had garages, which meant that there were a good many parked cars.

Mr. Giles, the headmaster at David's school, was always going on about crossing the road, or rather about not crossing the road except by the lollipop man.

'The road is so straight, you see,' he'd say. 'The traffic speeds up it and doesn't expect to find children jumping out from between parked cars.'

It isn't really straight though,' thought David. From where he was standing he could see it bent to the left a bit by the rec. Round the bend where you couldn't quite see, the nice houses started. They had bigger gardens and were semi-detached, not terraced: quite a lot of children from school lived in them.

David walked slowly up the road thinking about his model. He was going to build a lighthouse with a light that really flashed. He'd had to change his individual project from football to the sea coast before Miss Lawson would let him do it, but it was going to be worth it.

Mr. Harris the caretaker had let him have a piece of hardboard, and he was going to paint that like sea first. Maybe he'd ask Geoffrey Wall to help him. He was a good painter.

'Watcha, David!'

'Oh, hello.'

'It was Chris Lambert, David's best friend. He was doing the model too.

'I've got the light bulbs. I nicked them from the Christmas tree lights last night.'

'Oh, fantastic, Chris! Do you think Miss 'll let us start this morning?'

'No idea. You know what women are.'

'Huh, don't I just!'

Miss Lawson was always on whistle on Mondays. So she unlocked the classroom door and let the children in as soon as she'd blown it.

Dave and Chris were at the front of the line.

'Hello, Miss. We've got our stuff.'

'Lovely, we'll have to see when you can fit it in.'

David didn't like the sound of that. It was a school where they didn't follow a time-table. Mr. Giles was always going on about it.

'It's a great privilege to come to this school, children, to learn from such a talented group of teachers. So don't waste your time.'

It was good because there was time to do things you were interested in, and the teachers were prepared to talk to you about anything. Miss Lawson even pretended to like football, which was more than David's mum did.

Even so David was anxious.

'Hope she hasn't a bee in her bonnet about a page of maths and writing a story before assembly,' he muttered to Chris. Chris pulled a face.

After she'd taken the register and collected the dinner money, and taken in the absence notes, and chatted to Mr. Watson from class five who'd come to borrow something, Miss Lawson was ready.

'Right, children. Four things I'd like you to do today. Now let me finish please,' said Miss Lawson as David was about to interrupt.

'A page of maths, read for twenty minutes, write a story and your individual projects.'

'Great!' said Chris.

'But,' said Miss Lawson, 'please do everything else and show me before you start your projects. Now for a few suggestions for your stories.'

'Oh, well, not too bad,' thought David. 'We should have all afternoon at least.'

In fact he and Chris worked so hard, that it seemed no time at all before Miss Lawson was saying,

'Line up for assembly!'

He collected the hymn book which he shared with Chris and joined the line.

'You can't stand there, David Holmes. I'm saving that place for Jeanette.'

'Oh, give over,' said David and gave Ann a nudge with his elbow. It was a bit more violent than he'd intended and she lurched against Kim in front, who in her turn fell against a table. A bit of a rumpus started and Miss Lawson came over.

'All be quiet,' she said, 'and stop fussing.'

'But Miss,' began Ann.

'Don't interrupt me, Ann. If you don't know how to line up by now, you'd better go back to the infants and learn.'

Miss Lawson always said that if there was any trouble when they were lining up.

'Right, Anthony, lead on please.'

Sometimes assembly was boring, and today was one of those days. David found himself thinking about his model again. He couldn't wait to get the flashing light fixed up. He was so busy thinking about it that he forgot to sing, and Mr. Watson came across and tapped him on the shoulder.

David didn't really want to get on the wrong side of Mr. Watson because he ran the football teams. David thought there was a very good chance of his being picked for the first team in the Autumn, and he'd played with them already. Still, one never knew. So he started to sing.

After the hymn there was a short prayer and then the children sat down for the notices. Mr Giles looked a bit cross.

'Oh dear,' thought David. 'One of his grumbling days.'

'I don't like to be always grumbling,' said Mr. Giles. 'But I'm afraid the litter situation is very bad again. The field is covered in sweet papers and crisp packets, and someone has left a number of empty coca cola tins outside the front entrance. I'm afraid that unless the grass is cleared by 12.15 no one will be allowed on it all week. Now Mr. Banks has a notice.'

Mr. Banks rose to his feet. He was very tall and a lot of the fourth year girls were in love with him. He wasn't soft, though.

'It's about the school trip to Wales,' said Mr. Banks. 'If possible I'd like all money in by the end of the week, and there will be a meeting for those going at Wednesday lunch time during first sittings.'

There were a couple of other notices. One about Needlework Club and one about the Swimming Gala, and then the children stood up and led out of the Hall class by class.

At lunch time Mr. Banks came and sat on David's table.

'Well, David, and are you looking forward to going to Wales? Only three weeks to go now!'

'Not half, Sir!'

'Have you been there before?'

'No, Sir.'

'Where do you usually go in the Summer, David?' asked Mr. Banks.

'Clacton, Sir. We rent a chalet there.'

'Do you like it?'

'It's great on the pier, you know on the amusements, but I don't reckon much to the town and the beach. Too many people, if you know what I mean.'

Mr. Banks laughed, then he started to talk to Carol Jones. She was very quiet and sometimes smelt. Mr. Banks was kind like that. He made every one feel important and grown up and didn't treat you as if you were likely to be a nuisance. David was very glad he was taking them on the school trip.

* * * *

'It's really great!' said John Harris. 'Where are you going to keep it so it won't get smashed up?'

'Miss said we can put it in the stock cupboard,' said Chris. 'And I've got Stephen to move some of her things so we can put it right at the top.'

It was lovely. The boys had got Geoffrey to paint the sea, and it was all blue and green, with white round the plasticine base of the lighthouse to show the sea was rough. The lighthouse itself was made of yoghurt pots glued on top of each other and was painted with red gloss paint because the ordinary school paint wouldn't stay on.

Chris had put a little glass paste jar on the top so that it covered the light bulb: this was the best part of all. You could either work the switch to make the light stay on all the time, or you could joggle the switch so that it flashed. At the moment they had it flashing.

'Tomorrow we're going to make ships for the sea, and Miss said if it was still standing at the end of the week we can show it in assembly.'

David began to disconnect the batteries and Chris found an old cornflakes box to put them in. Then very carefully they carried the model on its piece of hardboard over to the stock cupboard.

It was a bit difficult getting it on to the top shelf and Miss Lawson came to help them. Even so it almost slipped and David was afraid it might end up a broken mess on the floor.

'Well, it should be safe there, boys. And now,' said Miss Lawson, 'I think you'd better be getting home or your mothers will be worrying.'

'All right, Miss. See you tomorrow.'

'Yes, see you tomorrow.'

As David walked past the rec. he saw Debbie playing on the swings. He waved to her and she came running out of the gate to meet him.

'Race you home,' he said.

He didn't really like people seeing him walking down the road with Debbie. He was half afraid people would think he was sissy. Still if they were running it wouldn't look so much as if they were together.

When they were half way home David had to stop to get his breath. He turned round and waited for Debbie to catch up.

'Come on, slow coach. Mum 'll have the tea on the table and no one there to eat it.'

But Mum didn't have the tea on the table. She wasn't even getting it ready. She was sitting in the old armchair in the back room all huddled up and their Auntie Madge was in the kitchen doing some washing up.

'Hello, Mum. You all right?'

'Yes, thank you, love.'

Auntie Madge came through and stood there looking odd. David thought she half looked as if she could smell something bad and half as if she was about to tell him off. Aunt Madge was a bit of a moaner and David had been on the wrong side of her before. Then she turned to his mum.

'Have you told them, June?'

His mum shook her head. Then she started to speak without looking at them.

'I don't really know what to say, but. . . .' And then she stopped again.

'Well, it's like this, and you might as well know now. Your dad's not coming back.'

'Why not?' said David. 'He's not – he's not dead, is he?'

'Be better if he was,' said Auntie Madge.

'Hush, Madge. No love, he's quite well. It's just that he won't be coming back here to live any more.'

David felt Debbie slip her hand into his. Suddenly he felt very responsible for everything.

'Mum,' said David, 'is it my fault? Is it because I scribbled on his pools coupon last week?'

'No,' said Mrs. Holmes. 'He still loves you both very much. You'll see him again. He just won't be living here, that's all.'

'Will you get a divorce, Mum?'

'Yes David, I expect so.'

'Geoffrey's parents have got one of those. His Mum went off with his uncle.'

All of a sudden Debbie burst into tears. She was trying to talk at the same time and tears were running into her mouth.

'I want my Dad,' she kept saying. 'I want my Dad.'

Mum took her on to her lap. She was crying a bit, too. David didn't know what to do. He looked from Mum's face to Auntie Madge's and back again.

He opened his mouth to speak, but his tongue had gone dry, so he swallowed hard.

'Will Dad ever come back to us,' he managed to whisper, 'or has he gone for ever?'

'For good,' said Mrs. Holmes. 'He said he'd gone for good.' Then she took out her handkerchief and blew her nose very loudly.

Chapter Two

It wasn't until Tuesday evening when he was lying on the floor watching the film on the telly that David remembered about the money for the school trip.

'Mum,' he said, not taking his eyes from the screen, 'Mr. Banks wants the money for Wales as soon as possible.'

'Oh yes, dear.'

'Do you think I could take it tomorrow?'

'I'm afraid you won't be able to take it at all. You see, love, we can't afford it now.'

David felt as if it was all a dream. Not afford it! Not go to Wales with all the others! It was unthinkable. He sat up and looked at his mother.

'But, Mum.'

'No "buts" about it, David. It'll be about six months before I really know how much we've got to live on, and until then we've got to be careful.'

'Oh please, Mum!' said David. 'I'll be ever so good.'

'Being good doesn't come into it, boy. We haven't got the money.'

'I'll go without my dinners, Mum. I could even get a job.'

'Now look here, David,' said Mum, 'that trip is only three weeks away. Try as we can, it's impossible to get the money. So I want to hear no more about it. I know you're disappointed, but please don't make it difficult.'

David felt awful then. The last thing he wanted

was to upset his mum. Even so, there must be some way round it.

'You'd better see Mr. Banks in the morning, David. In fact I'll write him a note now.'

'Oh, thanks, Mum. Don't say why we can't afford it though, will you?'

'No, not if you don't want me to.'

David went to see Mr. Banks after register the next morning. He wanted to get it over with before the lunch hour meeting, so that Mr. Banks didn't ask why he wasn't going in front of every body else.

Mr. Banks read Mrs. Holmes' letter carefully and then said,

'I hope you don't think I'm being nosey, David, but if your family can't afford to let you come to Wales, the school could pay a bit to help. Anyhow, tell your mum and dad and let me know.'

David didn't know what to reply to that. He knew he very much wanted to go, and he also knew his mum wouldn't like accepting money from anyone else.

'Thank you, sir. I'll tell Mum, but I don't think it'll help. You see, my dad's just left and she's a bit upset.'

'I quite understand, David, and thank you for telling me, but perhaps your mum could have another think about the school camp. Anyhow, tell me definitely by next week.'

David thought about what Mr. Banks had said all through the day. Somehow he knew his mum wouldn't let the school pay for him to go. She was funny about that sort of thing. Yet at the same time he knew he simply had to go, and this seemed to be the only way. He decided at last that there was no harm in trying, and that he'd wait until his mum was in a good mood.

The moment came later that day while they were having tea. Auntie Madge had gone home and there was just Mum, the girls and himself.

Mum had done spaghetti on toast and had bought some lovely frozen cream cake and a block of fudge ice cream.

'It's because I don't want you children to think this is a black week, what with school and Auntie Madge and everything.'

'I like school though,' said Debbie.

'I saw Mr. Banks this morning, Mum.'

'Oh yes, dear?'

'He was very nice. He said it didn't matter about the money. I can still go.'

'Don't be so silly, David, you can't go for nothing.'

'No, I know that. He said the school would pay.'

'What! You mean they'd give you the money? Why on earth should they?'

'Well, Mr. Banks said if children can't afford to go, the school will help.'

Mrs. Holmes' face went very funny. David thought she was going to cry, but instead she shouted at him.

'If you've told Mr. Banks about your dad, I'll never be able to go up to that school again. You talk too much, David Holmes. I'm too upset to think about money and school trips. I said you can't go and that's that.'

David said, 'O.K. Mum,' and got on with his tea.

That wasn't the end of it, though. After tea he went up to his room to finish painting a model aeroplane, and Alison came in.

'Honestly, David. I don't know how you could.'

'How I could what?'

'Say that to Mum about the money. You know how worried she is.'

'I thought it would be all right. It wasn't my fault she went through the roof. I want to go to Wales more than anything else in the world.'

'Huh, I thought you said you were a Christian.'

'I am. What's that got to do with it?'

'It should make you more thoughtful to Mum, not just wanting things for yourself.'

David knew that Alison was right, but he didn't want her to know that. So he said, 'I was being thoughtful. I'd found a way to get the money.'

'In the Bible, in the ten commandments, it says that you should do what your mum and dad say. I know it does 'cos we did it in R.E. yesterday, and our Mum said you can't go, so that's that.'

'It would be good for me to go, though. It's part of school. The teachers say it's good, and they can't be wrong, can they?'

'Well Mum's decided, so it doesn't matter much whether it's good or bad!'

'I do want to go Alison. And anyhow you can't talk about God and the Bible 'cos you're not a Christian.'

'Oh, shut up.'

Alison went out and slammed David's door. He knew that she'd got one of her moods on now.

David wished his dad was home. He'd have soon made a joke about it all, and then played a game or something. Dad was fantastic at games, and he liked making models too.

Just then, Mum called up the stairs,

'David, your turn to wash up.'

'O. K., coming, Mum.'

David fiddled about for a bit longer with his 'plane. He zoomed it round the room a few times, taking care not to damage the wet paint. Then he landed it gracefully on top of his chest of drawers.

'David, will you come down,' shouted his mum. Her voice sounded as if all the words were in capital letters. David recognized the danger signs and hurried down the stairs.

'Sorry to keep you waiting, Mum,' he said. 'But I was just at a tricky bit with my 'plane.'

When he'd said it he knew it was a lie. He felt especially bad when his mum smiled and said,

'Never mind, love, washing up always waits.'

So he said, 'Actually, Mum, I was flying it on practice runs.'

'That was nice, dear. Don't forget the saucepan.'

The children didn't usually wash up, but Mum had burnt her hand on the oven earlier in the week and had to keep it out of water.

David swished the cutlery through the water. He hated cutlery. The ice cream bowls were the best because you could pretend they were boats and jet bomb them with the dish cloth. He'd once done that with a glass dish and it had broken and cut his hand. So he only did it with the plastic ones now.

Debbie came out to help him dry up.

'Will you help me with my homework, David?'

'What homework do second-years have?' laughed David.

'It's for the student. She wants us to cut out pictures of animals from magazines. It's for our topic. We're going to the zoo next week.'

'How much does it cost?'

'Fifty pence and some more money to spend.'

'You going?'

'Of course.'

David left the sink and went into the front room where his mum was doing the mending.

'Mum, did you know Debbie's going to the zoo next week?'

'Yes, dear.'

'How much pocket money is she having?'
'Thirty pence, if she's good.'
'So that's eighty pence you're spending on her altogether.'
'Yes, David.'
'That's not fair.'
'What's not fair?'
'She's getting money for her trip and I can't have it for mine.'
'There's a bit of a difference between eighty pence and eleven pounds, isn't there?'
David ignored that,
'She's always spoiled, Auntie Madge says so.'
'And Auntie Madge says you're rude, so which would you rather be?'
'It's not fair. . . .'
'David! If I hear you grumble once more about that school trip in my house, I'll send you away to live with Auntie Madge, so that she can teach you some manners.'
'Sorry, Mum,' David mumbled and went out into the kitchen again.
He knew his mum didn't really mean what she said about sending him to Auntie Madge, but he still felt awful. He felt awful because he kept upsetting his mum, and he felt awful because he wanted to go to Wales and couldn't.
Debbie had finished off the wiping up by the time David got back, and was standing on the stool putting the plates away in the cupboard over the sink. She had to stand on tip-toe and the stool looked very wobbly.
'Here, let me do that, Debbie. You'll break your neck if you're not careful.'
'What did she say then?'
'She said you could go and you're having thirty pence pocket money if you're good.'

'That's ten pence more than Sally.'

'You're lucky then.'

'Shall we have a biscuit, David?'

'Better ask Mum first.'

'All right.'

Debbie ran in to ask and David looked round the kitchen. Now that his dad had gone he thought he ought to do something to help. His dad had always got the coal in when he was home, but they didn't need it in the Summer. So instead he emptied the kitchen bin into the dustbin. When he'd done that, he noticed there were some bits on the floor so he got out the pan and brush and swept them up.

'That should please Mum,' he thought as he looked round the tidy kitchen. Then he thought for a moment and shut his eyes.

'Dear Lord,' he said, 'I am sorry for upsetting Mum and being rude. Please make it up to her. This is David Holmes speaking. Amen.'

He felt better after that, and was even whistling when he went into the front room.

'Can I go out on my bike, Mum?'

'Yes love, don't be too long.'

'No. Bye.'

David went out again through the kitchen. He closed the back door quietly and walked down the garden. His bike was in the shed at the bottom.

It was just an ordinary bike, red and white, but David quite liked it. It was second hand and he knew his mum had gone without a new dress so that he could have it. Deep down he'd have really liked a chopper, but they were a fantastic price.

He wheeled it through the back gate and scooted the bike along the alley. When he got out on the road he turned and cycled up to the rec., which was where he usually met his friends in the evenings. As he passed the railings, David could see the boys playing football. They had to use sweaters for goal posts, because the real ones were taken away in the Summer.

David rode in through the gate and laid his bike down on the edge of the pitch.

'Hiya,' he called.

'Come on,' shouted Gary.

It was a good game. They weren't always, especially if people argued about what was a goal and what wasn't. But this time it was a good game.

They had to finish when the sky began to get dark. So they picked up the bikes and sweaters and went to sit on the swings. They decided to play Truth or Dare.

'Who's going first?' said Peter.

'The youngest,' said Gary. 'Then the next youngest and so on.'

Tony was the youngest and he chose a Dare. He was only eight, so they made him go and ask an old man sitting nearby what the time was.

Gary was next and he had a Dare as well. He had to ride his bike round the field with his arms folded. He wasn't too successful and fell off half way round. He didn't hurt himself too badly, only bruised his knee. Even so it took him several minutes to hobble back to the swings.

It was then David's turn. He decided to have Truth, partly because he almost always chose Dare, and partly because he had an idea that Jimmy Noon was going to ask him to ring someone's doorbell and run away. His dad had told him off for that only last week.

'Truth,' he said.

The other boys got together for a minute, then Gary said,

'Is it true your dad's gone off with another woman?'

David was furious.

'Who says he has?'

'True or not?'

'It's none of your business.'

'True or not? Come on, play the game.'

Then David didn't know what he was doing. He went for Gary and knocked him off his feet. Then he started lashing into him with his fists; he didn't care how much he hurt him. After a few moments the other boys pulled them apart. Gary had a nose bleed, and his shirt was all muddy from where he'd been rolling on the ground. David had a cut lip which was beginning to swell and one of his ribs felt a bit bruised.

'I hate you, Gary!' David shouted. 'You stinking coward!' And he tried to hit Gary again, but the other boys were holding him back.

'Let me go!' screamed David. 'Let me go.' He yanked his arms free.

'I hate you all. You yellow sissies. Get off me. Leave me alone.'

The tears were streaming down his face, he couldn't really see where he was going, but he managed to pick out his bike. He just wanted to get away now.

He pushed the bike down the path. The boys just stood and watched him go.

David felt very lonely. He had no friends now. Mum had told him off, he'd argued with Alison and Dad had gone. It really wasn't fair. It was too much bad to happen to one person. It was all Dad's fault too, and God's for letting it happen.

'I hate God,' thought David. 'I hate everyone.'

After David had put his bike in the shed, he crept very quietly up to the back door. Although the light was on in the kitchen, there was nobody there and David could hear the sound of the telly from the front room. He was half way up the stairs when his mum called out.

'Is that you, David?'

'Yes, Mum.'

'Aren't you coming in to say goodnight?'

'In a minute, Mum.'

There were sounds of a chair being pushed back, and within seconds his mother was standing framed in the doorway.

'Goodness me, boy. What have you been doing now?'

'Fell off my bike.'

'Come into the kitchen and let me see.'

David didn't say much while his mum was washing his face. He couldn't really, because she'd stuck a lump of cotton wool in his mouth. He didn't want to either – he didn't like telling her lies. He couldn't say what had really happened. Now he'd calmed down he couldn't help thinking about what Gary had said.

'Mum.'

'Yes, love. There, almost done now.'

'Where's Dad living?'

'In London.'

'Is he on his own?'

His mum breathed in deeply. She looked a bit embarrassed.

'No David, he's with one of his friends.'

'Oh, he's not lonely then?'

'No he's not lonely.'

'Can I have some milk, please?'

'Yes. I think I'll have some, too.'

David thought about his dad again when he was in bed. He did hope that he wasn't lonely.

'Dear Lord,' he said. 'I'm sorry I said I hated you. I don't really. Please look after Alison and Debbie and Mum, and our dad who's in London. Goodnight from David Holmes.'

Then he turned over and went to sleep.

Chapter Three

It was Sunday morning. David was lying in bed staring at the ceiling. He was trying to decide whether to get up and go and help his dad make the tea when he suddenly remembered that his dad wasn't there.

It was a horrible feeling, like when it flashed in your mind that you'd got to go to the dentist or your pocket money had been stopped.

'Wonder what Dad's doing now, at this very minute,' thought David. 'I wonder if he's thinking about me.'

He didn't have time for any more wondering though, because Alison banged in, carrying a cup of tea.

'Wake up, dozy,' she said. 'Shift up and let me sit down.'

'Where's Mum?'

'Having her tea in bed. I think she wants to be alone.'

'Don't talk daft, you sound like one of those women in sloppy films.'

'Thanks!'

'Any time.'

'Are you going to your Sunday Club?'

'S'pose so. I didn't go last week.'

'Mum said we're going to Auntie Madge's for lunch.'

'Oh great, that's all I need.'

They could hear Mum moving about in her bedroom. Then she called to them from the landing.

'Breakfast in a minute, you two. Hurry up and get dressed.'

David drank down the last of his tea,

'Where's Debbie?'

'Playing in the garden, I think. She's been up for ages already. Look, I must go and get dressed. See you in a minute.'

'O.K.'

When David had finished dressing he began to look for his Bible. He'd need it if he was going to go to Sunday Club, because it meant an extra point. One for going yourself, one for a Bible and one for taking a friend.

'That's funny,' thought David, 'I'm sure it was here somewhere.'

In the end he found it under a pile of comics at the bottom of his bed.

He felt a bit guilty about that because Mr. Shaw who was in charge of Sunday Club said it was a good thing to read your Bible every day and David knew he hadn't read his for ages.

'Still, I don't much like reading anyhow,' he thought.

'You look nice, Mum,' said David when he got downstairs.

'Thank you, love. Auntie Betty came in and set my hair last night when you'd gone to bed. Needed doing too, it felt terrible.'

'Is there any peanut butter?'

'What, for breakfast?'

'Yes I fancy it somehow,' said David.

'Well it's on the shelf behind the apricot jam.'

'Thanks, Mum.'

'Did Alison tell you we're going to Auntie Madge's today?'

'Yes.'

'Who's talking about me?' said Alison as she

came into the room.

'Mum was saying how untidy you were.'

'Get on with you, David,' said Mum. 'Go and call Debbie in for her breakfast will you?'

'Now,' said Mum, when they had all finished eating. 'We really ought to set out by twelve o'clock because we'll have to go by bus.'

'Is it all right if I go to Sunday Club?' said David. 'I'll hurry home.'

'Yes love,' said his mum. 'And I think you ought to change your trousers. They are a bit grubby.'

'Sarah Turner's asked me along to listen to records this evening, Mum. Do I have to go to Auntie Madge's?'

'We'll be back in plenty of time, Alison. Now please don't start to grumble. It's very kind of Auntie Madge to ask us at all.'

David slipped into the church hall a few moments late. He'd been held up at home by the breakfast washing up, and changing his shorts, and Debbie wanting her bike brought round. So that by the time he'd finally got out of the house he wasn't in a very good mood, and to make it worse when he had knocked at Chris Lambert's house his mum had said,

'Sorry, David, he's gone on. He thought you weren't coming this week.'

'Well, I'm here now,' thought David, as he slid into the back row next to Brian Sargent.

David hadn't been going to Sunday Club for very long, only about six months. Mr. Shaw was the leader of the Cub pack which David belonged to, and when he'd told the Cubs about Sunday Club David had joined straight away.

It wasn't like Cubs though. There were girls in it for a start, and quite a bit of singing. Apart from that it was good. They had quizzes and filmstrips and then they divided into groups and did work sheet things with a teacher.

David thought the best bit was when they heard about Jesus. He sounded a smashing person. David had decided to become one of his followers shortly after he had joined Sunday Club. They were called Christians.

He'd told his dad when he'd got home, but Dad hadn't really understood because all he had said was,

'That's nice, son. Can you slip down the road and buy me some cigarettes.'

When David had sat down, he had a good look round to see who was there. Chris was sitting a few rows in front with the rest of their gang. They were all speaking to him again now. They'd made up the morning after the fight.

After the notices, Mr. Shaw went up on the platform and took a blanket off something that had been standing in the middle of the stage. It was a small table with a telephone on it, and lying next to the telephone something which looked like a garden cane. Mr. Shaw picked up the stick and waved it around. All the children laughed because on the end was a silver star, and Mr. Shaw looked so ridiculous standing in front of them all with the wand held high.

'I'm not a fairy godmother,' said Mr. Shaw smiling. 'No one can have three wishes when I wave my wand.'

Then he put it down on the table again, and looked a bit more serious.

'Some people,' he said, 'some people think that praying is a bit like waving a wand and asking for all your dreams to come true. They think God will give them anything they want. They think he's only there to be asked for things. They're wrong, prayer isn't like that at all. It's more like using a telephone.' He picked up the receiver, putting it to his ear.

'Well,' thought David.

'Prayer's like using a telephone,' went on Mr. Shaw, 'because it's like talking to a friend who you can't see. We can't see God, but he's a friend who will listen.'

* * * *

They had to wait twenty minutes for the bus and when they did finally get on it, it went so slowly that David thought it would have been quicker to walk.

Auntie Madge lived on the other side of town, and they had to change buses in the city centre:

'A bit of a drag,' thought David, 'just for something to eat.'

On the second bus, he and Debbie went upstairs and sat on the front seat. David wound the the window down, which made you feel as if you were in a sports car, if you kept your eyes closed.

'Now what's going on here? Shut that window, son, or we'll all be blown to kingdom come,' said the conductor.

'Oh sorry,' said David.

'Don't do it again, that's all.'

'Can't have any fun, can we, Debbie?' said David.

'Never mind, let's count red cars.'

'It's not worth it, we're nearly there, worse luck.'

'Don't you like Auntie Madge?'

'Not much. Why, do you?'

'No, but I like the rabbits.'

David had forgotten about the rabbits, and about Uncle Bert. He was Auntie Madge's husband.

People always seemed to forget Uncle Bert, who was short and thin, and going a bit bald. He never said very much. David thought he seemed almost frightened of them. His mum just said that he wasn't very good with children.

'He's good with rabbits though,' thought David. 'Maybe he'll let us play with them.' But he didn't hold out much hope. Uncle Bert didn't really trust children.

'Come on, David, we're here,' shouted Debbie, and they swayed along the top of the bus towards the stairs. David just managed to grab Debbie in time to stop her falling down the stairs as the driver slammed his brakes on.

'Hurry up, you two,' shouted Mum. 'The bus can't wait all day.'

Auntie Madge's house was just round the corner. It was very like their own house, but in a quieter road.

Auntie Madge herself answered the door.

'Come in, do,' she said. 'Perhaps you children would like to sit in the front room until the meal is ready.'

There didn't seem to be much choice, so they went in.

'And don't climb on the furniture,' said Auntie Madge.

'As if we would,' thought David.

The three children sat down. Alison took an emery board from her bag and started to do her nails.

'I hate it here,' she said. 'It's like a prison.'

David knew what she meant. All the walls seemed to be close together. The furniture was large and dark and the curtains were always half drawn to keep out the sun.

'I hope she isn't going on at Mum,' said Alison.

'What do you mean?'

'Auntie Madge has never liked Dad. She was having a go when she came over last week.'

'What's meant to be wrong with him?' said David.

'Oh, you know, he's not serious enough, all that sort of thing.'

'I think he's all right!'

'He's the best dad in the world,' said Debbie, and burst into tears.

'Oh, be quiet, Debbie,' said David. 'Or Auntie Madge'll start on us next.'

It wasn't a very pleasant lunch. The food was eatable, if you liked soggy cabbage with your roast lamb and lumpy custard with the apple tart, but Auntie Madge just didn't stop talking. It wasn't about Dad, although she did hint now and then, but mostly about the neighbours. Anyhow it was very boring.

Uncle Bert only opened his mouth once, and that was to ask for the salt. Mum said 'Yes' and 'No' in the right places and the rest of them just sat. Then Auntie Madge focused her attention on Alison.

'And what, my dear, are you going to do when you leave school?'

'I don't know.'

'You don't know! I thought your mother said that you were going to be a hairdresser.'

'Well, I might. I'm not leaving for three years yet.'

'And David, how are you getting on at school?'

'All right, thanks.'

'And what's your favourite lesson?'

'Topic, I think.'

'Topic! What on earth's that?'

'A mixture of things really. Something you're interested in.'

‘Oh, I see,’ said Auntie Madge. ‘Would you like some more custard?’

‘No, thank you.’

After lunch Debbie was allowed to go and look at the rabbits. Alison and David did the washing up. They had just finished, and were about to slip out of the back door when Auntie Madge caught them.

‘Now don’t go out there. Bert can’t manage all three of you. You’d better come and sit with us.’

So they did and it seemed absolutely hours before Mum said, ‘Well, Madge, I think we ought to be going. Thank you very much for putting up with us.’

‘That’s all right, Jean,’ said Auntie Madge patting Mum’s shoulder. ‘At a time like this we all have to make little sacrifices.’

* * * *

Somehow the journey home felt shorter. It went quickly for David anyway, because he had another good idea on top of the bus. He mentioned it to Mum when they got home.

‘Mum,’ he said, ‘you know Auntie and Uncle haven’t any children.’

‘Yes, David.’

‘Well does that mean that they’ve got more money than us?’

‘Yes, I suppose it does,’ said Mum, ‘but that’s none of our business.’

‘Do you think though . . . Well, wouldn’t it be a good idea for us to borrow some money from them?’

‘I hope that we won’t ever need to, David.’

‘If we did though, Mum, if we did I could go to Wales.’

‘No,’ said Mum. ‘Once and for all, no.’

Chapter Four

They had the road up outside Benstor Junior School the next morning, and the lollipop man was having an argument with the workmen.

'You'll have to move them lights,' he said. 'Or I can't get the children across the road, can I?'

'Now look 'ere, mate,' the workman was beginning. 'Now look 'ere.'

David and Debbie were waiting to be crossed over.

'We'll be here all day,' said David. Then he saw the lollipop man's stick and thought about Mr. Shaw and the magic wand and the telephone.

'Dear God,' he said in his mind, with his eyes open in case the lollipop man called them over. 'This is David Holmes speaking. Please don't forget that we want our dad back and I would like to go on the school journey,' and as that sounded a bit rude he added, 'Thank you for my breakfast.'

'Stop dreaming, David, we can cross now,' said Debbie, tugging his arm, and they ran across the road while the lollipop man held up the traffic.

When they arrived in the playground, the whistle still hadn't gone, so Debbie went to play on the apparatus and David joined in a game of flicks with some boys from the fourth year. He was sorry he did because he lost ten cards and only won two. He hoped he'd win them back at lunch time.

Mr. Banks was on duty and as David was going in he called him over.

'Has your mum thought any more about the school journey, David?'

'She says I can't go, sir.'

'Oh, I see. Well I'm sorry but I'm afraid, David, that I'll have to give your place to someone else. Maybe you'll be able to come next year.'

David walked off towards his classroom. Well, that was it, he wouldn't be able to go now. There would be no room, even if his mum did manage to get the money.

'A lot of good praying does,' thought David, as he kicked a crisp bag which someone had left lying on the floor.

When he reached the classroom, Miss Lawson was reading the register. She looked up as he opened the door.

'Sorry I'm late, Miss Lawson. Mr. Banks wanted to see me.'

'Thank you, David. Remind me that I want to speak to you after register, will you?'

'Oh what's happened now?' David thought, and, 'Yes, Miss Lawson,' he said.

'It's your model, David,' Miss Lawson explained five minutes later. 'I wonder whether you and your friends would like to show it to the school in assembly. If so, perhaps you had better go and set it up in the hall now, but mind Mrs. Green's P. E. lesson, will you. I've had a word with her and she says it's all right for you to work in there.'

'Oh thank you, Miss! Do we have to say anything?'

'You could explain how it works and how you made it.'

David went off to collect the other boys, and they went over to the art end of the classroom, where their completed lighthouse was now displayed.

David thought it was the best thing he had ever done at school. The others had helped, of course, but it had been mostly his idea and it had worked out even better than he'd hoped.

'All we need to do is carry a couple of tables into the hall and put it on that,' said David. 'Then check everything's working properly.'

They were soon organized, and apart from one of the tables catching Marion Smith in the back, there were no accidents.

It took quite a long time to check the model out though and the boys were very thorough. It would be awful if one of the battery connections came loose just as they were going to show it all to the school.

They tried to whisper, but Mrs. Green had to tell them to be quiet twice.

'We'd better go back to the classroom,' whispered Chris. 'And decide who's going to say what.'

'Don't let's write it down though,' said Geoffrey, when they got back to their room, 'or I'm bound to get muddled up when I read it out again.'

They all laughed at that.

'We don't have to say very much, anyway,' said David.

When it came to assembly time, Miss Lawson told the three boys to sit next to their model. They felt a bit conspicuous there, because it meant they were out in the front facing the rest of the school. David felt sure everyone was looking at him. It was terrible.

After the hymns and prayers were finished, Mr. Giles told everyone to sit down.

'Our assembly has a slightly watery flavour this morning,' he said. 'First of all I have some swimming certificates to give out.'

There were about ten and the children had to

come out to the front to receive them. One girl tripped as she came past the boys, and almost fell on to the model. Chris and David stared furiously at her, but she didn't seem to notice. Geoffrey made sure that everything was still working.

'And now,' said Mr. Giles, 'a group of boys from Miss Lawson's class have something to show us. Over to you boys.'

They stood up and David began. At first he felt a bit nervous and got in a muddle, but he sorted himself out and in no time at all he had finished his bit and Chris took over. When they had all three finished speaking they connected the battery so that the light flashed.

Mr. Giles thanked them very much and told the school to lead out.

During the day several people came up to David and told him how much they liked his model, and at lunch time one of the teachers asked him where he had come across the idea. He began to feel quite important.

In fact he felt pleased with himself all day, until home time when Chris said,

'Have you got all your stuff for Wales yet, David? My mum said she was going to buy me a new parka today.'

'Oh,' said David as he started tying up his shoe-lace, 'I thought I'd told you.'

'Told me what?'

'I can't go now.'

'Why not?'

'Mum says we can't afford it – my dad's – my dad's not at home now, you know.'

'Yes I know.'

'S'pose I thought Mum would change her mind. But even if she did it's too late now. Mr. Banks has given my place to somebody else.'

'Bad luck, David,' said Chris, not looking him full in the face. 'I'll miss you.'

David couldn't say anything to that. He was beginning to feel like crying again. So he closed his mouth and breathed hard. He felt as if nothing good would ever happen to him again.

'I counted on God making it come right,' thought David. 'Those prayers haven't done much good.'

And that was just what David said to Mr. Shaw after Cubs the same evening. David thought that Mr. Shaw ought to know. He'd hate God to let him down as well.

'You know that talk we had on Sunday, Mr. Shaw.'

'Yes David,' said Mr. Shaw. 'Here, help me move these chairs will you? Now what was it you were saying?'

'Well, it doesn't work.'

'What doesn't work?'

'Praying doesn't. I prayed for two things and they haven't happened.'

'Maybe God thinks it's better for you if you don't have the things. . . .'

'They're not selfish though. I did want to go on our school trip, and that's half work, and now Mum says no. And our dad's left home. I want him back for all of us. I did pray and he hasn't come. There isn't even a letter.'

'Oh,' said Mr. Shaw, 'I see. Well I suppose it's not much help saying that God knows best, is it? But when you're praying, David, do you ask God for a long list of things, or do you talk to him like you do to me or your friends? Think about it. God's your friend, you know, not Father Christmas. Now we'll just move this table over and then I think it's all tidy. Thanks for staying to help. See you on Sunday.'

'Yes, bye sir.'

David wheeled his bicycle home because he wanted to think a bit. He really had hoped that God would sort things out for him, and here was Mr. Shaw saying he was going about it all wrong. Maybe God didn't want him to go to Wales, and maybe he didn't even want Dad to come back, which seemed very strange because after all he was their dad. By the time he reached the alley, David felt completely muddled. He didn't really understand about God and praying, and he couldn't go back and ask Mr. Shaw again. It was too late. But he felt that he had to do something, so he said,

'Before I forget, thank you for being my friend, God,' though putting it like that did sound a bit wet.

Mr. Jones next door but one was weeding his onions when David went past.

'Hello lad, been to Cubs, have you?'

'Yes. It's great.'

'I was one when I was a lad.'

'Oh yes.'

David couldn't imagine that, somehow. Mr. Jones was about as old as his granddad.

'Well, goodnight boy. Keep up the good work.'

'Yes. Night, Mr. Jones.'

David let the gate bang behind him, which started the dog off at number seven. Debbie leaned out of the bedroom window.

'Bring me up a drink of water, David.'

'Where's Mum?'

'Auntie Betty's.'

When David had delivered the water, he went downstairs again into the front room. Alison was doing her homework.

'Mum said bed at nine. She's gone to Auntie Betty's.'

'Yes, I know. Can I have the telly on?'
'All right.'
'Is Mum having her hair done again?'
'No, she's gone to get something from Auntie Betty's catalogue.'
'Thought we hadn't got any money.'
'I think she wants some sheets. If you remember you put your foot through one last week.'
'Oh yes.'
'There I've tried,' said Alison. 'Stupid work. I shall be glad to leave.'
'Do you think you'll really be a hairdresser?'
'Hope so. I'd like my own shop, you know with people to do the customers' nails and faces, as well as hair.'
'You can't afford it.'
'Not straight away, silly. When I've earned some money after my training.'
Alison was almost grown up, or so she said. David wondered if she knew anything about praying. He had to get it sorted out.
'Have you ever prayed, Alison?'
'Yes, I used to, but it never worked. Why, do you?'
'No, well, not very often. It should work, shouldn't it, if you do it properly?'
'Yes. I suppose so. Do you want some cocoa?'
'Yes please.'
'Well you'd better get ready for bed first or you won't half catch it.'
David thought about Alison as he went up the stairs. He hadn't expected her to know what to do about praying, but she hadn't even been interested. She didn't seem to care much about Dad going either: not like Mum who had a cry when she thought no one was watching.
Mum came in while David was in the bathroom.

He could hear her laughing.

'Oh, you have to laugh,' Mum was saying as he came downstairs.

'What at, Mum?' said David.

'Your Auntie Betty, she's that funny. Had me in stitches she did. She said she'd knit you that jumper, Alison.'

'Oh great!' and she and Mum went on talking about jumpers and clothes and sheets.

David tried to watch the television, but it was only the news. Then a good detective story started. David sat very quiet and hoped his mum wouldn't notice, but she had built in radar or something because as soon as the titles had finished, she stopped talking to Alison and said,

'Come on David, bed time. Don't hang about, please.'

'All right,' he said, 'give me a chance. Night, Mum, see you in the morning.'

Chapter Five

At the end of the afternoon Miss Lawson always read the class a story. Usually she chose a book which she thought they'd like and read a chapter or so every day, so that it took about three weeks to get through a whole book.

This time she'd chosen an animal story. David thought it was awful. They'd had a whole week of it now and he was sick to death of it.

'Stupid,' thought David. 'Wish we didn't have to listen.'

Miss Lawson made them sit there, though.

'If you don't like the story,' she said, 'sit and think of something else, but please don't disturb the rest of us.'

'All very well for her,' thought David, 'but it's jolly difficult to think with someone reading all the time, and girls sitting near you. I wonder how Chris is, though.'

Chris had gone home early. His mum had taken him to the optician's.

'Hope he'll be allowed up to the rec. this evening,' thought David.

Chris's mum was a bit fussy about things like that.

'I suppose I could try talking to God now . . . Maybe praying will work today.'

So he did. He told God all about the school journey and how he couldn't go on it, and then he went on to his dad. He told God all the details, how horrid Auntie Madge was and how they all wanted their dad back. He knew that God knew about it all already, but that didn't seem to matter somehow.

'I don't want you to do anything particular this time,' David finished up, 'just what you think is best (though I do want my dad back).'

David felt much better then,

'Well, it's up to him now,' he thought.

He realized that Miss Lawson was still reading, and it still sounded soppy.

David felt in his pocket for his football cards. Yes, they were still all there. He just stopped himself from getting them out. If Miss Lawson had seen those, they would have been torn up and in the bin in next to no time. She used only to throw the cards away, but one day she'd caught Jimmy Tyler taking some out of the bin again. So now she always tore them up first.

'Can't see why teachers don't like them,' thought David.

He kept his hand in his pocket and tried to count the cards. The first time he made it twenty six, and the second time twenty eight. It was a bit difficult, and he was afraid the cards would spill out on to the floor. Then he felt the purse that his mum had given him with the shopping list in.

'Don't lose it, David,' she'd said. 'There's a fifty pence in it. I've got to go out today, so I thought you wouldn't mind doing this bit of shopping on the way home.'

'Wonder where she's going, she didn't say.'

Miss Lawson's voice interrupted his thoughts.

'Right now, children. Walk out quietly please. See you in the morning.'

David walked down the road with Geoffrey as far as the shops. Geoffrey couldn't wait for him because he had to collect his sister from the infants.

'Bye, David, see you tomorrow.'

'Yes. Bye.'

David pushed open the shop door which rang a bell somewhere out the back. He went up to the counter and pulled out the purse with the list in. He had to wait to be served because there was another lady in front of him.

His mum had told him to give the list to Mrs. Jackson, but he wanted to read it out himself. It seemed more grown up.

'Well what can I do for you, lad?' asked Mrs. Jackson.

'Please can I have a packet of orange jelly, a tin of spaghetti and a pound of sugar.'

'What sort of sugar, David? Here let me have a look,' and she took the list from him, spread it out on the counter and put on her glasses. Then without saying any more, she went scurrying round the shelves fetching the items.

David felt annoyed. That was typical of grown ups, he thought. They didn't give you a chance.

'And how's your poor mother?' said Mrs. Jackson.

'All right,' said David. 'At least she was this morning.'

Mrs. Jackson gave him a funny look.

'She's had a hard time, you know.'

David said, 'Yes,' but he felt angry inside. His mum and dad weren't other people's business.

Mrs. Jackson wrapped up the things.

'Well there you are, son. Now mind you don't drop it. I've put the change in the bag.'

'Thank you very much,' said David as he walked out of the shop. The bag was quite bulky, so he decided to take it straight home. He had to hold it at the bottom, too, in case the things fell through, so by the time he arrived home he had pins and needles in both arms.

His mum opened the door before he got there. She must have been in the front room and seen him walk past.

'Here we are now. Let me take those from you,'

she said. 'There's an ice lolly for you in the fridge.'

'Thanks, Mum.'

'And your comic's come.'

'Oh, great.'

At tea time Mum told them her good news.

'What do you think?' she said. 'I've got a job.'

'Oh have you, Mum, where?' said Alison.

'In a shoe shop down the main road,' Mum said. 'It's only part time, so I can be back for when you get in from school, and I don't have to go in on Saturdays.'

'What about holidays, Mum?' said Alison.

'Well, I told the manager I'd wait and see,' said Mrs. Holmes. 'Maybe we can arrange it so I go in a few days a week, but that's a long way off.'

'Have you got to go to work, Mum?' said David. 'For the money, I mean.'

'Well love, it'll certainly help. But it'll be nice to meet people, and to get out of the house a bit more.'

After tea Mum got out her sewing.

'I start on Monday,' she said. 'So I thought I'd get ahead with a few things while I can.'

It started to rain, so David played with Debbie for a while instead of going out. He soon got tired of her though, and went up to his bedroom to sort out his comics. He began to think about Mum's job. If only she'd started a week earlier, he might have got his money for the school trip.

Then the 'phone rang and his mum called up to him.

'David. It's for you.'

He ran downstairs. He thought it was probably Chris. He often rang David in the evenings. But it wasn't.

'Hello, son,' the voice said. 'How are you?'

'Dad!' whispered David, then he couldn't think of anything else to say.

'I was wondering,' said Dad, 'whether you and Debbie would like to come out with me on Saturday. Alison can't come, I know. I'll take her out another time.'

'Oh,' said David.

'I've asked your mum, son, and she says it's all right. I'll pick you up at about 10 o'clock.'

'I'll remember, Dad,' said David.

'We'll have our lunch out, so don't bother about sandwiches,' said Dad.

'Will it just be the three of us?' David didn't want any of Dad's friends spoiling their day.

'Yes. See you on Saturday then. Can I have a word with Alison?'

'Hold on. I'll go and get her.'

Alison was on the 'phone for what seemed like hours, chattering away and laughing. Then Dad spoke to Debbie. He didn't speak to Mum again, only those few words when she'd answered the 'phone.

'What'll you do on Saturday, Mum?' said David when they were all having their hot drinks before they went to bed.

'Will you be all right?'

'Oh yes, love, thank you. Think I'll go over to Madge's for the day. Pity Alison couldn't go with you, isn't it, but she'd promised to go up to town with Pat Earles and her Mum.'

'I don't mind,' said Alison. 'Dad said he'll take me out on my own next week.'

'I wonder where we'll go?' said David.

'Told me he'd let us choose,' said Debbie. 'I'd like to go to the zoo. . . .'

'Thought you went yesterday with the school,' said Alison.

'I did, but I'd like to go again. It's ever so good there, you know.'

'I don't mind going there,' said David. He thought anywhere would be good with Dad.

It didn't seem right though, Mum being left at home, and Dad not talking to her properly on the 'phone.

'Will Dad take us out every week, Mum?' Debbie was going on.

'Yes, love, most weekends, and in the holidays you can go and stay with him.'

'What, where he's living now?'

'Yes, or maybe he'll take you away somewhere.'

'Smashing!' said Debbie.

'I wish he could live here now,' said David.

'Well it's just not possible, I'm afraid.'

'Have you got a divorce then?' David had heard somewhere that divorces were final, like dying.

'No, not yet, but we're thinking about it.'

'Oh,' said David.

Then Debbie started wondering what she could wear, and Alison had another go at Mum about using nail varnish. David thought it was almost as if they'd forgotten Dad.

He thought about it all in bed that night too. He just couldn't get to sleep and kept thinking about Mum and Dad and why it all had to happen.

'Funny though,' he thought. 'I did talk to God about it this afternoon, and already two things have happened. Mum getting a job, and Dad ringing me up.'

He turned over in bed. He just couldn't get to sleep, so he decided to have another word with God.

'This is David Holmes speaking, God,' he said. 'Thank you for my Dad ringing up and for my Mum getting a job. Please go on doing what's best, but don't forget I want my Dad home. Goodnight, God.'

Chapter Six

David couldn't wait for Saturday to come. It was only two days to go, but it felt to him as if time had stood still.

Miss Lawson told him off several times.

'If you got on with your work, David Holmes, time would go faster,' she said when she caught him staring again at the clock. So David did, and when lunch time finally came, he felt it had been the longest morning of his life.

So he tried to forget all about the outing to the zoo, and pretended that Saturday was going to be a very ordinary day, which was all right until he remembered what was really happening, then he felt all excited inside, as if worms were crawling about in his stomach.

On Friday night Mum made them wash their hair and clean their shoes really properly. She even let Debbie have some bath salts in her bath water. When David went in to say goodnight, he could smell them.

'You smell funny, Deb. What is it?'

'It's special. It's Mum's Heavenly Night. Do you think Dad will like it?'

'No, not much.'

'Oh you. . . .'

She pretended to be annoyed, but David knew she was laughing inside.

'David, do you think Dad will look the same?'

'I should think so, it's only a fortnight since we saw him last.'

'Oh yes, I forgot. It seems longer doesn't it?'
'Yes.'
Then Mum came upstairs and told them it was time to go to bed.
It did seem much longer than a fortnight since they'd seen Dad, thought David as they were waiting for him next morning. He and Debbie were sitting on the wall outside the house waiting for Dad's car to come. They weren't really sure which direction he'd be coming from, so they looked one way and then the other.
Then David decided he wouldn't look up the road again until fifty cars had gone by, but in the end he counted to a hundred and there was still no Dad.
'Run in, Deb, and see what the time is,' said David.
'What if Dad comes while I'm gone? I'll miss him.'
'He won't if you hurry.'
'You go then.'
David didn't really want to risk that, so he stood on the front path and shouted in at the front door.
'Mum! What's the time?'
'Don't shout, David. What do you want?' said Mum who was only in the front room.
'What's the time?'
'Er, let me see, twenty-five to ten.'
That meant Dad was late. He'd said he'd come at half-past nine and now he was late.
'Maybe it's the traffic,' said David.
'Hope he hasn't forgotten,' said Debbie.
'Don't talk rubbish.'
All the same David knew it was no good. He knew Dad wasn't coming for them. But he went on sitting on the wall. There didn't seem to be anything else to do. He began to feel very odd inside, not ill exactly, more a kind of nagging ache. David

tried to ignore the thoughts which kept buzzing round his head. But it was no use, there was no escaping it. Dad had let them down. Then Debbie banged him in the back.

'He's here!' she shouted. 'He's here!' And sure enough there was Dad's firm's car, with Dad in it pulling up in front of them. Dad waved, then got out. He walked round to the pavement.

'Hello,' he said. 'Feel like a day out, do you?'

'Hello, Dad,' said David, smiling so much he felt his face would crack.

'Hello, hello,' shouted Debbie, jumping up and down and clutching Dad round his waist.

'Run in then and tell your mother we're off,' said Dad. Mum was in the kitchen.

'Bye, Mum, Dad's here and we're off now.'

'Bye love, have a good time. Behave yourselves.'

'Yes.'

David rushed back up the hall. Dad was back in the driver's seat and Debbie was in the back. He got in beside her and shut the door.

'Where's it to be then?' asked Dad.

'Oh, the zoo please,' said Debbie.

'All right then. Hold on tight.'

And they were off, down the street towards the town. Past a'' the shops and the bus station where they'd caught the bus for Auntie Madge's, and on through the suburbs to the city.

Dad looked different somehow. David couldn't think what it was at first. Then he realized.

'Coo, Dad, you've got a moustache.'

It wasn't very long, but it did make Dad look strange, sort of foreign.

'Do you like it?' said Dad, fingering it. 'I'm still growing it, of course.'

'Makes you look like someone on the telly,' said Debbie.

And it did too. Dad had a new sweater on as well.

A purple one with a polo neck, and when David moved his head he noticed that Dad had different trousers.

He hadn't changed really though. He soon had them laughing. He'd make a joke of anything, Dad would.

'How's the old bag?' he asked. Dad always called Auntie Madge that, not to her face of course, just to make them laugh.

'Awful,' said David. 'Moan, moan, moan.'

'She means well though,' said Dad, which was funny. That was what Mum always said.

They stopped at a garage for petrol and Dad bought them a packet of sweets each.

'To keep you going,' Dad said, 'until lunchtime.'

By the time they'd got to the zoo the car park was quite full, but Dad managed to squeeze the car in somehow: he was a good driver.

Then they crossed the road and Dad bought the tickets at the gate. Debbie of course wanted to show them all around.

'This way,' she said, grabbing Dad's hand. 'Let's go and see the elephants first and then the penguins.'

'Hang on,' said Dad. 'We'll plan this out properly. We don't want to miss anything.'

So he bought a plan of the zoo from the ticket office and marked out a route in pencil.

'When we get to here,' he said, 'to the monkeys, we'll knock off for a bit of lunch.'

In almost no time it seemed that they were sitting in the café, eating their lunch. It was a self-service place, and Dad let them have just what they wanted. In the end they all had sausage and chips and ice cream, 'And three cokes,' said Dad to the lady behind the counter, 'we're celebrating today.'

'I liked the lions best,' said David as he ate up his sausage. 'Wouldn't it be awful if one escaped?'

'Oh don't,' said Debbie, and looked round as if she expected one to walk in the door that very moment.

'Tell you what,' said Dad. 'We'll go to a Safari Park next time. They have lions and tigers walking about almost wild there.'

'Oh, can they get at you?' said Debbie.

'No love, you drive past them in the car. They can't get you unless you open the windows.'

'When can we go?' said David.

'Next time I take you out if you like,' said Dad, 'and now I think we'd better plan our route for this afternoon.'

When they got to the insect house, Debbie held very tight to Dad's hand.

'Do we have to go inside?' she said. 'I didn't when I came with the school.'

'Oh, this is the best bit,' said David. 'Come on, Debbie, there's nothing to be scared of.'

'Oh all right,' said Debbie, but she didn't look very pleased.

'It won't take long,' said Dad. 'And don't you go frightening her, David.'

So David didn't open his mouth. He just walked along from one case to another, with his face right up against the glass. The spiders were fantastic, especially the hairy ones. He was sure he'd seen one of the ones marked poisonous in his back garden. If it was still there, perhaps he could find it and send it to the zoo and make a fortune.

'Had enough yet, David?' said Dad. 'Think we ought to be heading back now.'

'Oh, Dad!'

But before they went back to the car, Dad took them into the zoo shop and said they could have fifty pence each to spend.

David bought a little ashtray with a picture of

the zoo on for Mum, and a postcard of some giraffes for Alison. With the money he had left he bought a book on spiders, and one of those plastic spiders that joggle up and down on elastic.

Debbie spent all her money on a teddy bear. She'd bought Mum something from the zoo when she'd been with the school.

Then on their way to the car Dad bought them all an ice lolly, which was just the thing they all wanted.

'My poor old feet,' said Dad. 'I don't think I can walk a step further.'

They all laughed. They knew Dad didn't mean it really. He was only joking.

On the way home David began to feel sick. Not the ill sort of sick, but the other kind. He didn't want the day to finish and his dad to go away again.

'Dad,' he said, 'why can't you come home and live?'

'Well, I've got another home now, son.'

'Why, what's wrong with ours?'

'You'll understand, I hope, when you're a bit older, but sometimes grown ups find they'll be happier away from each other. Mum and I thought it was best.'

'But you're married,' said Debbie, 'and there's us, we want you to stay.'

'Well, I'll put it simply,' said Dad as he put the car into gear and turned a corner. 'I want to live with you children. Mum wants to live with you children but the problem is that Mum and I aren't happy together. So she's looking after you, because she's better at cooking and washing than me, and I'll visit you as often as I can.'

'Don't you love Mum any more?' asked David.

'I'm very fond of her,' said Dad. 'But it's no good. I can't come back.'

'Oh,' said David.

Then Dad told them about the flat he lived in now, and made them laugh about the pekinese dog who lived downstairs.

After that they played the racing driver game, and made racing car noises when Dad went round corners.

Before they knew it Dad was driving down their street and they were home again.

'I won't come in,' said Dad, 'and I'll ring you up in the week. Be good.'

'Bye, thanks for a smashing day,' said David, getting out of the car. Debbie kissed Dad, then slithered along the back seat, and got out on the pavement side.

They stood outside the front gate and waved until the car had gone round the bend in the road. After that it all seemed a bit flat as they walked up the front path and banged on the door.

Mum let them in. She was just doing the ironing, she said, and had they had a nice day? They told her all about it, and David gave her the ash-tray.

'Why, it's lovely,' she said, 'I'll put it on the mantelpiece in the front room.'

They had tea sitting round the telly because it was Saturday. Debbie spent the whole time telling Mum about the zoo.

'And Dad's got a moustache now, Mum,' said Debbie. 'He looks ever so handsome. And David made me go in the insect house.'

That reminded David of the spider. So when tea was finished and washed up, he went out in the back garden to look for one.

The poisonous one he'd noticed last week under a rose bush didn't seem to be around any more.

'Still it can't have gone far,' thought David. 'I'll set a trap for it.'

So he fetched a biscuit and crumbled it up under

the bush, and made a little trail into an empty jam jar. He couldn't think how to trap the spider once it had got inside the jam jar, but he decided that if it was comfortable enough, it might make a nest there. So he put in some bits of grass and leaves for its bed.

When he'd finished he had a last look round, just in case the spider was lurking anywhere, then went inside to warn the others.

'I've got a spider trap in the back garden,' he said. 'Don't move it, will you, Mum?'

'Where is it, love?'

'Under the rose bush.'

'Oh,' said Debbie. 'How horrible!'

'If you're going out again,' said Mum, 'p'raps you could give the plants a little water. The ground's that dry. The watering can's in the shed.'

David found the can, and filled it with water from the kitchen tap. He kept well away from the rose bush. He didn't want his spider to be drowned to death. When he'd filled and emptied the can three times, he got a bit bored with it all and went to put the can back in the shed. It was very untidy inside, with deck chairs and step ladders leaning all over everything. Dad kept his tools on the shelf. David glanced up and they were still there! The nails and screws in old tobacco tins, and the saws and drills hanging on hooks.

Dad wouldn't have left home without his tools, not for good. Dad loved those tools, and he used to spend hours out in the shed making things.

'That's one good thing about your dad,' said Auntie Madge. 'He's clever with his hands.'

David leant against the side of the shed and thought about it all very carefully. It just didn't seem to make sense. He couldn't believe that Dad would ever leave home for good without his tools.

So that meant that Dad must be coming back. It must mean that one day Dad would walk in through the front door, calling out to them just as he always used to.

David decided not to tell the others about it. He'd let Dad surprise them.

Chapter Seven

David told God about Dad and the tools later that evening, when he was playing with his plastic spider in the bedroom. Mum wouldn't let him have it downstairs.

'Sorry I haven't talked to you for a few days, God, but I've been very busy,' said David inside his head. Then he decided that he couldn't really say that because God knew everything.

'Well, actually I forgot,' said David, 'but I've something important to say now.' And he told God all about finding Dad's tools.

'I wouldn't mind so much about the school trip,' David finished off, 'if you could manage to make Dad come home. Goodnight from David Holmes.'

David kept his secret about Dad's tools for three days. It was quite difficult because he was sure that people could see he had a secret.

'What are you smiling about, David?' Mum had said to him at breakfast. 'You look as if you've won the pools.'

On Thursday afternoon Dad had picked Alison up from school and taken her out for the evening. David was still awake when she came home. He looked out of the window to try and catch a glimpse of Dad, but it was almost dark and all he could make out was Dad's car pulling into the middle of the road.

So he waited until he heard Alison come upstairs, and then crept out on to the landing.

'Was it good?' he whispered.

'Yes. I'll come in and tell you,' she said. So they both went into David's room. David climbed back into bed and sat with the covers pulled up over his knees. Alison sprawled out on the bottom of the bed. She looked very grown up, David thought.

'We went to the pictures first,' she said, 'and then we had a meal at a real restaurant. It was smashing, the waiter called me madam!'

'What did Dad say?'

'What about?'

'Oh nothing. Well, did he say anything about coming home?'

'Of course not, silly.'

'I'm not silly, so there. I know something you don't. I know he is coming home.'

'He's not,' said Alison.

'Well,' said David, 'if you think you're so clever I'll tell you something. He's left his tools in the shed, and he'd never do that if he wasn't coming back. I know.'

It sounded a bit silly now that he'd actually told Alison, and he knew she wouldn't think the tools were very important at all.

'I expect he just forgot them,' said Alison, 'but he can't come home, David. He's going to marry somebody else.'

'You're a liar,' shouted David, giving Alison a punch on the arm.

Then Mum came in. She was very cross.

'You should have been asleep ages ago, David Holmes,' she said. 'And I told you to go straight to bed, Alison. I'm very annoyed with you both. Stop sulking, David, and go to sleep. Come on, Alison, bed.'

Then she went downstairs and David heard her out in the kitchen. He felt as if nobody cared about

Dad at all and he couldn't remember when he'd ever felt so unhappy.

Things didn't seem much better the next day. He couldn't get up, and when he did, he couldn't find his swimming things.

'They're where you left them, I suppose,' said Mum, who was trying to get ready for work. 'I don't remember seeing them anywhere, love.'

In the end he had to go without them. He only just got to school in time and then he found his things had been at school all the time. But they were damp and soggy because they hadn't been hung out to dry.

David kept thinking about what Alison had told him. He didn't really believe it. Dad wouldn't marry anyone else, he was certain, but Alison had been so sure about it all.

He didn't manage to get much work done and Miss Lawson made him stay in at lunch time to catch up. That was awful because the classroom was empty except for Miss Lawson doing some marking, and David just couldn't concentrate. Then Mr. Banks came in, and he and Miss Lawson started laughing and joking. David felt sure they were laughing at him.

At last home-time came. David thought he'd never been so pleased to get out of the classroom.

When he arrived home, he dumped his bag and swimming things on the kitchen table and went out into the back garden to inspect his spider trap. He'd looked every day since he'd put it there, and he'd renewed the biscuit crumbs, but he hadn't caught anything.

'Maybe they don't like biscuits very much,' thought David, and he looked round to try and find some greenflies or ants to use as bait instead.

'What are you doing?' said a voice behind him,

as he had his head under the rose bush. It was Alison.

'Looking for spiders,' said David.

'I'm sorry about last night,' she said, 'but Dad's ringing you tonight, so you can ask him, can't you?'

'S'pose so,' said David, then he brought his head out from under the bush.

'It's wrong though, isn't it?'

'What is?'

'To have two wives. It's against the law.'

'Well, he won't have two at once, silly. He's divorcing Mum first.'

David thought hard. He couldn't understand why Dad had to upset everything. It had been all right before. He could feel he was going to cry. He couldn't understand what was happening to him, he seemed to be getting more like a silly girl every day.

Mum called them in for tea then, so he didn't have a chance to say anything more to Alison. Then just as he'd got a piece of cake almost to his mouth the 'phone went.

'Can one of you go?' said Mum. 'Your legs are younger than mine.'

'I will,' said David. He liked answering the telephone because they hadn't had it very long, and anyway it might be Dad.

'Hello,' said David. 'Buryford 3739.'

'Hello, son,' said Dad, 'guess who!'

'I saw your car last night,' said David.

'You should have been asleep, my lad.'

'Yes, I know.'

'Look, David, I can't manage Saturday this week, but can you all come out on Sunday afternoon?'

'I think so. I'll ask Mum.'

He ran back into the kitchen.

'It's Dad on the 'phone,' he said. 'Can we go out with him on Sunday afternoon?'

'Yes, I should think so. Ask him what time, will you?'

David rushed back again.

'Yes that's all right, Dad, what time?'

'Oh about twoish, I should think. We'll go to the Safari Park shall we?'

'Oh yes.'

Then David remembered what he was going to ask Dad, but he didn't feel he could somehow. It seemed a bit rude. After all, Dad was a grown up. So instead he asked Dad about the tools in the shed.

'No I haven't forgotten them, son, but I haven't got room to keep them here, or anywhere to use them. You'll have to look after them for me.'

David couldn't say any more because Debbie had come up. She was hopping about waiting to speak to Dad.

'Hurry up, David,' she whispered. So he said goodbye to Dad and handed the 'phone over.

Mum was the last person to speak to Dad. When she came back, she looked as if she were about to cry again.

'I'm seeing Dad again tomorrow night,' she said. 'He's coming round late, after you've all gone to bed. We want to sort a few things out. You must all be very good and not come down. Now let's finish eating, shall we?'

After tea he and Alison did the washing up. Mum's hand was still bad.

'Well what did Dad say, then?' asked Alison. David picked up a saucer and began to wipe it.

'I didn't ask him. Didn't like to really, not about getting married anyway. But I did tell him about the tools. He said that I could look after them for him.'

'Oh, I see. I should think that saucer's dry by now. Hurry up a bit. I want to go and see Pat – we're going to do our homework together.'

After the washing up David went out for a ride on his bike. He went up to the rec., but none of his friends were there, so he just rode round for a bit before going home. One day he was going to go a long way on his bike, maybe on a Saturday so that he needn't rush too much. He wanted to go right out into the country.

'I won't tell Mum though,' he thought, 'she'll only say I'm too young.'

When he woke up the next morning he didn't feel at all well. His nose was blocked up and his throat hurt. He tried to speak but only a funny noise came out.

'Five, four, three, two, one, testing,' he croaked. Then he got out of bed and staggered into Mum's room.

'I don't feel very well,' he said.

'You don't look it either,' said Mum. She was sitting up in bed combing her hair.

'Come here and let me look at your throat. Er, it's all red, back to bed with you for now.'

After Mum had got the others off to school, she brought David some breakfast on a tray.

'It's cold milk and scrambled egg,' she said. 'That'll slip down easily. Now, I've been round to Auntie Betty's and she'll bring you your lunch in. I can't miss a day at work already. You'll be all right, won't you?'

'Yes, Mum.'

'There's a bed made up on the settee, so you can go down and watch the telly if you want. Now I've written down Betty's 'phone number for you, just in case. See you about three, love. You'll soon be feeling better.'

Once Mum had gone and David had eaten his breakfast he did feel a bit better. He felt quite important being left on his own.

After a while he went downstairs, but it was only a schools' programme on the television, so he turned it off again. There didn't seem to be very much to do.

He went out into the kitchen, and there was a note on the table, ICE CREAM IN THE FRIDGE it said. So he took it out and cut a slice from the block. Lovely and smooth on his throat it was, as he licked it off the spoon. It made an interesting sucking noise.

'I know,' thought David, 'I'll write a letter to Dad.'

He went to the drawer where Mum kept her paper and envelopes and he found a biro under the newspaper on the table. He sat down and thought hard.

'Thursday,' he wrote. 'Dere Dad I am at home ill with a cold. I hope you are well, Auntie Betty is bringing my diner becos Mum is at werk. I have got a spider trap in the garden, but havnt cort anything yet. See you on Sunday. Love from David.'

He folded it up and put it in an envelope.

'I must be stupid,' he said to himself, 'I don't know Dad's address. Maybe Mum does.'

After the letter writing he felt a bit bored, so he went back to bed with a comic, but it didn't seem to help much. He felt like someone to talk to. Then he remembered God. He had quite a lot to say to him again.

'Hello, God,' he said, 'things here are getting worse. Alison says that Dad's going to marry someone else. I do wish you would stop him.'

David didn't really think that God was doing much to help. If God waited much longer, Dad would be married and it would be too late.

'I know Alison and Debbie want Dad back here as well as me,' David went on, 'and anyway we need him.'

The front door banged,

'Cooee,' called Auntie Betty, 'it's Auntie Betty; can I come up?'

'Of course,' David called back, 'and goodbye God,' he said, 'I must go now.'

Auntie Betty came in the room.

'How's the invalid?' she asked.

'Oh, a bit better thanks.'

'I've brought my dinner round, too; thought you'd like a bit of company. Do you fancy some shepherd's pie?'

'Oh, yes please.'

'Come downstairs then. You'll be all right if you wrap up warm.' And she made David put his dressing gown on, even though it was Summer.

'Who's been at the ice cream then?' said Auntie Betty as she saw the saucer and spoon in the middle of the table.

'Well I had a little slither this morning, but not very much.'

'You'll be as fat as a house boy,' she said laughing.

David liked Auntie Betty. Her children were grown up, but she wasn't that old. She wasn't really their Auntie either, but they'd always called her that. She'd lived round the corner for as long as he could remember.

After lunch they went into the front room and Auntie Betty got her knitting out. She was making a sweater for her husband. She put the telly on for David and there was an old film on. It was quite good, too, about the American Civil War.

In no time at all Mum was back again.

'Oh thank you, Betty,' she said. 'Hope he hasn't been any trouble.'

'No,' said Auntie Betty, 'I've enjoyed it.'

'I feel better too, Mum,' said David.

'Well we're all happy then,' said Mum. 'I'll go and make a cup of tea. I'm simply parched.'

Mum didn't sound happy later on though. Dad came round at about half-past nine as he'd promised.

David could hear them talking downstairs. Every so often their voices were loud enough for him to almost hear what they were saying. He was sure they were quarrelling. When he left, David heard Mum calling Dad horrible things, and then the front door slammed and it all went very quiet.

In the morning Mum told them she and Dad were definitely getting a divorce – they thought it was the best thing.

Chapter Eight

Alison was having a good old moan on Sunday afternoon.

'It's not fair, Mum,' she said. 'It would have to happen to us.'

The rain was pouring down outside. Water streamed down the kitchen window, and rain drops dripped off the rose bush into the spider trap.

'Dad 'll never come in weather like this.'

'I expect he'll come,' said Mum, 'but I'm sure I don't know where you'll go.'

'Not to the Safari Park and that's for sure,' moaned Alison again.

'Why not?' shouted Debbie and David together.

'If you think we're traipsing about looking for animals in this weather, you've got another think coming,' shouted Alison back.

'Now don't start, please,' said Mum. 'I'm sick and tired of hearing you children argue. Go and do something quiet until your dad comes.'

When Dad did come, Debbie answered the door.

'Where's Mum?' said Dad.

'Upstairs washing her hair,' said Debbie, 'shall I get her?'

'No don't worry, just tell the others we're off and give Mum a shout.'

'All right.'

They decided where to go when they were in the car.

'I'm afraid the Safari Park's off,' said Dad. 'Is there anywhere else you fancy?'

'Can we go to your flat,' asked Debbie, 'and see what it's like? We could have tea there.'

'Not today, love,' said Dad. 'It's not really convenient.'

'I don't want to go there anyway,' said David. Maybe the lady Dad was going to marry would be there and he didn't want to meet her.

In the end they went to one of those big houses that was open to the public. David didn't think it was all that interesting, but the girls did. But still it was worth it to be with Dad.

First of all they drove up a long avenue between trees and then parked on some gravel near the house. They had to make a dash for the front door, as it was still bucketing down.

When they got inside the hall, Dad paid for the tickets and bought a guide book for Alison. David thought it was rather boring, but there were one or two good bits, like the armour and the guns which were hung on a wall.

'Wonder if anyone still lives here, Dad?' said Alison.

'I think so, love, in the parts that are private.'

'I wish we could live here too,' said Debbie.

'No one to play with,' said David. It was miles from the nearest house.

After they'd been all the way round they ran back to the car again, and then went to have tea in the village nearby. David thought that was the best part.

'Now eat up,' said Dad. 'You must be hungry.' So they all did. David ate the most. He had bread and jam and two big pieces of chocolate cake and an ice cream.

'Oh I feel sick,' he said when he'd finished. 'It's lovely.'

But it was Debbie they had to stop for when they were on the road again.

'I feel awful,' she said, 'can you stop please?'

'Just as you say, lady,' said Dad.

'Oh hurry up, Dad,' said Alison, 'I've got a new skirt on.'

Dad pulled up just in time. He made Debbie stay out in the rain and take deep breaths.

'It's better to have a wet person in the car,' said Dad, 'than the other thing.'

They all laughed except Debbie, who didn't think it was very funny at all.

'You'd better sit in front, Debbie,' said Dad.

Nobody talked much as they got near home.

'Can you come in for a bit, Dad?' asked David as they turned into their street, 'just for a few minutes?'

'I'm afraid not, son. I must be getting back. I'll see you next week.'

The girls kissed Dad goodbye and climbed out of the car.

David stayed inside.

'Dad,' he said, 'will you ever come back?'

'No, David. I keep telling you, lad, I'm never coming home.'

'But your tools.'

'Not even because of the tools. Now, David, please believe me.'

David clambered out of the car and slammed the door. He rushed off down the road. The rain didn't matter any more. Tears were streaming down his face, and he made funny choking noises.

He was crying because he felt Dad didn't want him anymore. Dad had chosen to go away and leave him.

'He's horrid,' thought David. 'He's spending lots of money on new clothes and going out when we need him at home. I hate him.'

He walked about for a long time and when he arrived home he was soaked through.

Even so David remembered to read his Bible when he got to bed and he told God about his day out. He told him out loud because it was easier to think what to say next.

Debbie came in just as he was finishing.

'Who were you talking to, David?'

'Oh nobody,' said David. Then he thought he'd better tell the truth. He didn't want Debbie to think he was daft.

'I was talking to God. He's my friend, you know.'

'Oh, does he talk back?'

'Not so you can hear.'

'Oh, a bit like when I talk to my dolls.'

'A bit, except God's alive, stupid.'

He didn't want Debbie to get the wrong idea.

'Is it the same as praying?'

'Well yes, I suppose so.'

'I'm going to bed now. I thought you were talking to Alison.'

'Night.'

'And goodnight God,' said David. 'Please don't forget about my Dad. His name is Frank Holmes. I'm sure you can make him come back to us if you really try.'

* * * *

'If you really try, David,' said Miss Lawson, 'you can manage this maths without my help, I'm sure.'

David was standing at Miss Lawson's desk. He hadn't felt much like maths.

'Now you read this to me and try and make me understand it.'

It wasn't that it was difficult, but it was sets, and David didn't like them very much. He thought they were silly. He read the page through to Miss Lawson.

'I think I understand it now, Miss.'

'Well go and attempt it and if you still can't do it, then you'd better come back.'

David went and sat down at the table by the window where he and Chris usually worked. He was on his own this morning though. Chris had gone to a meeting for the school trip, so had Geoffrey, and Gary was still away.

'Must have been cut badly on Friday,' thought David, 'or just putting it on.' He'd fallen off the swings in the rec. and his head had bled for ages.

David read his maths page through again and began to write down the answers. A whole week the others would be in Wales. A whole week, to say nothing of the endless meetings Mr. Banks had, and if it hadn't been for Dad he'd have been going too.

David was trying very hard not to mind about the trip now that it was nearly here. He didn't mention it any more at home and when Chris and Geoffrey talked about what they were going to do he tried to look interested, but it was very difficult.

His pencil rolled off the table and on to the floor, and when he picked it up he discovered the lead was broken. And as he walked over to the pencil sharpener, Miss Lawson started on him again.

'Now what's the matter, David? You're up and down like a yo-yo.'

'My pencil's broken, Miss Lawson.'

'Oh well when you've sharpened it perhaps you could manage to do some work.'

David went and sat down again. Chris and Geoffrey didn't come back for nearly half an hour and when they did get back he had still hardly started his maths.

'Move along, David,' said Chris. 'You're taking up all the room.'

Then Chris and Geoffrey showed him the notebooks Mr. Banks had given them. On the first page they'd written down the places they were going to every day.

'Looks smashing,' said David.

'Wish you were coming,' said Chris.

'So do I,' said David. 'So do I.'

Mr. Banks had meetings for the school trip on the next two mornings as well. He explained about the journey and told the children what sort of things they'd be seeing on their days out and the kind of work he was expecting from them.

Geoffrey and Chris were more excited about the trip every day. They couldn't talk about anything else. In the end David was so fed up that he didn't sit next to them on Wednesday afternoon. He felt awful because they were his best friends.

'What's the matter with you?' said Chris, when he passed David's table.

'Nothing,' said David, 'just leave me alone.'

He did go over and talk to them both at the end of the afternoon though. . . .

'Hope you have a good time,' he said. 'See you next week.'

The trip was leaving very early the next morning. By the time school started they'd be half way to Wales.

'We'll send you a postcard,' said Chris. 'Don't work too hard.'

David felt so fed up that he even let Debbie walk home with him. He didn't care what people thought any more. She was jabbering on as usual. David didn't take much notice of what she was saying.

'Well, do you?' shouted Debbie.

'Do I what?'

'I've asked you three times already. Do you think Dad will 'phone tonight?'

'I don't know,' said David. 'I can't see into the future.'

'He said he'd 'phone this week,' said Debbie, 'and it's Wednesday already.'

'Well maybe he will then,' said David. 'I don't care.'

'Oh that's an awful thing to say. I'll tell Mum.'

'Go ahead!'

He gave Debbie a little push. He didn't mean to hurt her, but she tripped over a ridge in the pavement and fell down. When David went to help her up she shouted at him.

'Go away. You're horrid, I hate you.'

Her hands and one knee were bleeding, and there was black on her face.

'You're the meanest boy there is.'

She was standing up by this time. David was going to say he was sorry. She really looked funny. Her face always went red when she lost her temper, but as he moved towards her she started shouting again.

'I'm going home to tell Mum. Keep away from me.'

Then she ran off down the road. David was going to run after her, but as she was nearly home anyway he decided not to bother.

'Stupid girls,' he muttered, and kicked a paper bag that was lying in the gutter. He walked slowly home. Might as well let Debbie have her say before he arrived. He didn't think Mum would be too pleased anyway. She wasn't.

'You're such a bully, David,' she said. 'Why you have to keep hurting your sister I don't know.'

'I didn't,' said David, 'she. . . .'

'Don't argue with me,' said Mrs. Holmes. 'Sometimes I feel I just can't cope with you all. I feel like sending you to Auntie Madge's. Go up to your room until tea time.'

David stomped up the stairs. No one, he felt, would give him a chance. When he got to his room, he pulled his chair over to the window and opened it as far as it would go. Then he knelt on the chair and leaned out. He felt as if he was in a prison. His mum didn't allow them to lean out of the windows.

'What happens if the sash cord breaks?' she would say. 'The window would come crashing down and have your head off. Anyway if you lean out too far you might fall.'

That was the trouble with Mum. She always saw trouble long before it happened.

David noticed Alison walking down the road with her friend Pat. They were laughing. Pat was showing Alison something written on a piece of paper. They stopped outside the Holmes' house and sat down on the wall. David couldn't really hear what they were saying. He climbed down from the chair and had a look in his toy box. He easily found what he wanted and went back to the window. He had a lump of plasticine in his hand which he divided into little pieces.

'Drop bombs now,' he said under his breath as he threw one of the lumps at Alison. It missed.

He hit her on the ear with his third shot, and quickly ducked below the window so she shouldn't see him. He hit Pat twice and Alison three times before they realised where the plasticine was coming from.

'Go away, David,' said Alison, 'and leave us alone.'

David sat down on the floor. Dad didn't want to come home; Mum wanted him to live with Auntie Madge. Alison thought that he was a nuisance and Debbie hated him. He felt miserable and alone, though deep down he was sure of one thing and that was that Dad still loved him.

It was about then that he had his good idea.

Chapter Nine

'Think I'll go to bed now, Mum,' said David at about eight o'clock. 'I feel a bit tired.'

'All right then. I'm going round to Auntie Betty's in a few minutes, but I won't be in late.'

When he reached his room, David put on his pyjamas just in case Mum came up to check, then he turned down his bed. Next, very quietly, so as not to make a noise, he lifted his suitcase down from its place on top of the wardrobe.

It wasn't really his. It was an old one of Dad's that David kept comics in, but it would do. He emptied it out and pushed all the comics under the bed. Then he started packing. He put in some clothes and his newest cars and his action man. Then just as he was closing the case, he remembered his Bible and put that in too. After he was packed he listened for Mum to go.

'Bye, Alison,' she said as she banged the front door. David could hear her heels on the pavement as she walked up the road. He went downstairs and looked in at Alison.

'I'm just getting a glass of water,' he said and closed the door.

In the kitchen he went over to the shelf where Mum put the letters. Sure enough there was a piece of paper with Dad's address on. David copied it out on the back of an old envelope. Then he picked up his glass of water and went upstairs again.

He didn't have much money in his cash box, but enough to get to Dad's, he hoped. He tipped the coins in the envelope with the address on and put it on the bed. Then he got dressed again, and put his pyjamas in the suitcase. He picked up the envelope and put that in his pocket. Then he pushed the pillow down the bed to make it look like a person and turned off the light. He could hear the television going downstairs. He opened his door and listened again. Debbie was breathing deeply. She'd left the door open.

He picked up his case and tiptoed out to the top of the stairs, then very slowly he started down them. It was much easier than he'd expected, and in no time at all he was out on the pavement: nobody had heard him.

He tried to walk normally along the road, as if he went for a stroll every evening with a suitcase. He felt that people were looking at him from every window. If they were, nobody came out and in five minutes he was on the main road. He turned right and headed down towards the station. It was about a mile, but he didn't want to risk anybody recognizing him at the bus stop.

The station was a main line one and David had decided to go right into London and ask the way when he got there.

He went over to the ticket office. The clock on the wall said five to nine.

'Single to Euston, please,' he said.

The man pushed the ticket over.

'Twenty pence, please. Bit late to be travelling on your own, aren't you?'

'I'm on my way home,' said David. It wasn't really a lie.

'Platform Five you want,' said the man. 'Down them stairs and it's right in front of you.'

'Thanks,' said David, and went the way the man had said.

There weren't many people on the train. So

David sat on a seat on his own. He looked out of the window. He hoped it didn't show but he was feeling frightened.

It was dark by the time the train came into Euston, and there were so many people. He got Dad's address out of his pocket. He hoped it was near the station. He had planned to ask the way from a ticket office man, but there were long queues in front of all of them. The other railway men seemed busy too.

David walked out of the station into the street. He knew that London was a huge place, but he was sure that someone would know where Dad lived.

He turned right and crossed over a big road. He had decided to ask the next person who passed about Dad's address, but all the people were in such a hurry, rushing past before he could open his mouth to speak.

Then he saw a man standing in a shop doorway. David went up to him and showed him the envelope.

'Excuse me, but do you know where this is, please?'

The man looked foreign; he had dark hair and a moustache.

'Not understand,' he whispered.

David turned away again. He walked on and on. He did eventually manage to ask several people the way, but none of them knew. One of the men had been drunk, and that had frightened David. The man had leant right down, level with David's face and his breath smelt strange.

'I don't know, sonny boy,' he'd said. His words had been very slurred, and difficult to understand.

David had twisted past the man and hurried off. He slipped down a side road, and when he thought it was safe he walked back to the main road again.

The case was now extremely heavy. It banged against David's leg every time he took a step and his hand hurt too. It was really night time now and not many people were left on the streets. David was very scared.

Then a car drew alongside him and a friendly voice said, 'Want a lift, son?'

David looked up. It was a police car. He knew that it would be safe, and he also knew that he would have to be very careful about what he said, in case the policeman took him back to Mum.

'Yes, please,' said David, 'but I'm not sure of the way from here.'

David told the man the address, which he knew by heart now.

'Well, that's not far,' said the policeman. 'Hop in.'

Once David was inside the policeman began to ask a lot of questions. It was awful because David didn't want to tell any lies.

'I'm going to stay with my Dad,' he said, 'and I lost my way.'

But the policeman went on and on. Asking if Dad was expecting him, and where his Mum lived. For a moment David thought that he was taking him to the police station. But then the car turned down a narrow street, and the man said,

'Here we are then. I'll wait until you're inside.'

Fortunately for David, the house where Dad lived had two doors. Anybody could walk into the first one, but before you could go through the next one, you had to ring the bell for the flat you wanted.

David heard the policeman drive away as the first of the two doors swung shut behind him.

There were five bells, and all of them had a name by the side written on a piece of paper. David looked for Holmes. It was the second one down.

'Almost there,' thought David as he rang the bell. But it rang and rang and no one came.

Chapter Ten

David didn't know what to do. It hadn't occurred to him that Dad wouldn't be there. He looked at the other bells and wondered whether to ring one of those and ask if they knew where Dad was. He decided not to in case the people made him go back to Mum and the girls, or even rang the police. He didn't want all those questions again.

Mum might have his picture on the telly by now saying he'd been kidnapped or something.

David gave his Dad's bell one more ring, just in case he hadn't heard, and when there was still no reply he went outside and sat down on the steps to wait.

It wasn't too dark in the street because the lamp posts were very bright. There weren't many people about. David huddled himself up in the corner made by the top step and the railings which ran down the side and hoped nobody would notice him. He laid the case down flat beside him and put his head on it. The last thing he heard before he went to sleep were cats fighting at the end of the street.

After a while a car pulled up and the driver got out slamming the door, and walked up the steps.

'What on earth . . .' he began. Then he saw who it was.

'David!' he said very softly and stooped down and touched the boy on the shoulders.

'Wake up, lad. It's your Dad.'

Dad picked up the case and held David's hand.

'Can you manage the steps, son, or shall I carry you?'

'I'll be all right now,' David yawned. 'Now you've come.'

Dad's flat was on the third floor. He unlocked the door and pushed it open.

'Here we are, lad,' he said. 'I think you'd better come in and explain.'

Dad told David to sit down, and went through another door where the kitchen was. He came back with a glass of milk.

'Drink that up first,' he said. 'Then start at the beginning.'

'I don't want to be any trouble,' said David, 'but I want to live here with you.' He told Dad about Debbie falling over and him being sent to his room, and Mum threatening to send him to Auntie Madge and then how he'd managed to run away. Dad pulled on his moustache and frowned.

'You can stay here tonight,' he said, 'and we'll talk about it in the morning, but I'm afraid you'll have to go home. Get undressed now. You can have my bed and I'll sleep on the couch.'

A few minutes later, when David was tucked up, Dad went out again.

'I'm just going to 'phone Mum. I shan't be very long,' he said.

David fell asleep at once. He didn't hear Dad come back from the telephone, or the man upstairs the next morning as he clattered about, getting ready to go on early shift. In fact he didn't wake up until his dad shook him by the shoulder and said,

'Wake up, son. Here's a cup of tea.'

When they'd finished breakfast they went on sitting at the table. It was a small one, poked in the corner of the kitchen.

'Aren't you happy at home?' asked Dad.

'No,' said David. 'I want you back. I'll be happy then, I promise.'

'We've tried to explain, David. I know it's hard for you. We're getting a divorce soon you know.'

'I don't want to. I want you home.'

David had been sure his dad would come if he knew how much they wanted him.

'No, lad.'

'Well, can I come here then? I wouldn't be any bother. I'd tidy up and everything.'

'There's not enough room, son.'

Then David felt as if something was bursting inside him. He wanted to cry and hit out and scream all at the same time. Dad didn't love him after all. He didn't want him to stay. Dad didn't care that he, David, was unhappy.

'I hate you. I hate you,' shouted David. 'You must let me stay, I've got nowhere else to go.'

He started to cry after that, and made such a noise that it was some time before he could hear what Dad was saying. When he had calmed down a bit, Dad made him sit down.

'Now listen to me for a moment,' said Dad. 'I love you, you're my son, I'll always love you. I do care about you David and I don't want you to be unhappy, but I can't come back.

'In any case,' Dad went on. 'I want you to be at home to look after Mum and the girls. They need you, you know.'

'What did Mum say last night?' said David. He'd forgotten all about Mum.

'She didn't know you'd gone until I rang, thank goodness. But she was very upset to think you'd been so unhappy and not told her.'

'Oh,' said David.

'But I told her you did what you thought was

right,' said Dad. 'I think she understood.'

'Dad,' said David, 'do you think you'll get married again to someone else?'

'Very likely,' said Dad. 'But that won't make any difference to you. I'll love you just the same and come and see you. When I get a new home, you could even come and stay with us. If you want to, that is. And now we'd better see about getting you back.' David wondered where Dad's friend lived. He'd almost forgotten about her. He was just about to ask when Dad said, 'Come on, lad, get a move on.'

David packed his case again. He hadn't needed much out of it, only his pyjamas and some clean socks. He rammed the pyjamas back on top of the Bible. He didn't feel God was being much help.

Dad washed up and put the couch straight. Then he picked up David's case.

'Off we go,' he said. 'Got everything you came with?'

On the way out of London, Dad stopped at a 'phone booth to tell them at work that he was having the morning off. He bought David some sweets and a comic at the same time.

David felt a bit better once they were moving. He was glad Dad hadn't been angry. And he wasn't looking forward to seeing Mum again. Dad must have known what he was thinking, because he said,

'Don't worry. Mum 'll be pleased to see you. She loves you very much, you know.'

There wasn't really any answer to that, so David just went on looking out of the window. They were nearly home. Dad said it would only take forty-five minutes, even though it was the rush hour.

When they did arrive, Dad came up the path

with David. He carried the case for him. Mum must have been waiting because she opened the front door before they got there.

'Hello, June,' said Dad, 'one traveller safely delivered!' And he handed Mum the case.

'See you at the weekend, son. Keep smiling.' He put his hand through David's hair, then walked back to the car.

'Bye, Dad,' shouted David after him.

'Come on in, love,' said Mum. She went into the kitchen and put some milk on for coffee. David followed her through. He didn't know what to say. He hoped Mum wasn't upset.

'I do love you, Mum, you know.'

'I know you do. Don't try to explain, love, I think I understand. I'm just sorry Dad and I have let you down.'

'You haven't, Mum. Honest.'

That was awful. Grown ups didn't apologize like that, not for big things anyway.

'Now let's forget all about it. The girls know you ran away, but they won't talk about it. Only, if you're unhappy again, do come and tell me and I'll see what I can do.'

'O.K. Mum.'

'Well, I've got the morning off work, and it's too late for you to go to school. So what shall we do with ourselves?'

They decided to make some fudge. David thought it would be a surprise for the others when they came home.

After lunch Mum made David go to school. She gave him a note for Miss Lawson which said he'd had the morning off because he hadn't slept very well which was true in a way. He hoped Debbie hadn't told anyone what had really happened.

As he walked up the road he felt he'd been away for years. He was quite surprised to see all the shops and houses were the same.

He was only just in time for afternoon school. The children were going in as he reached the playground. Gary was back. He had a big plaster over the cut on his head, where he'd cut himself in the rec.

'Wonder how the others are getting on in Wales,' he said to David as they lined up at the door.

'Having a smashing time, I expect,' said David. 'They're probably there by now.'

Miss Lawson opened the door,

'Come in quietly, please,' she said. 'Glad to see you back, David, have you got a note?'

When Miss Lawson had settled them all down to work David went up to her desk.

'Please could I go along to my sister's class?' said David. 'I've got a message for her.'

'Yes, certainly,' said Miss Lawson, 'as long as you don't stay chatting.'

David thanked her and went towards the door.

'Wait a moment, David,' called Miss Lawson. 'Could you give this list to Mrs. Griffiths while you're there please.'

Mrs. Griffiths was Debbie's teacher. She took the list from David, read it through, and scribbled something on it.

'There, you can take it back again now,' she said.

'Could I speak to my sister first, please?'

'Yes, she's over there in the corner.'

David crept over to where Debbie was standing, choosing a library book. She had a bandage on one knee and a plaster on the other. David had forgotten about pushing her over.

'Hello,' he said, 'thought I'd come and tell you I was back.'

'Oh David,' she said. 'I am glad. Please don't run away again. It was horrid. Alison and I cried this morning.'

'You're daft, that's why,' said David. He was glad she'd missed him all the same.

'Mum and I made you a surprise this morning,' he said. 'Hope you like it. See you later.'

David gave Miss Lawson back the list when he got back to the classroom. Then he sat down with his maths. He wanted to finish it by home-time.

'This fudge is smashing,' said Debbie, as she ate the last piece.

'Hope it doesn't bring out my spots again,' said Alison, 'I was just getting rid of them.'

'Can I make some too, Mum?' asked Debbie.

'P'raps at the weekend, dear, but I haven't enough sugar in at the moment.'

'And you need vanilla essence,' said David. 'We used the last drop.'

'By the way,' said Mum. 'Auntie Madge is dropping round tonight. I haven't told her about last night. Probably best not.'

'What's she coming for?' asked Alison.

'To be company for me,' said Mum. 'She said she'd cheer me up.'

'Huh,' said David.

'I'll try and keep her out here,' said Mum. 'You children can go in the front room with the telly.'

Auntie Madge didn't stay long. 'She said she had to go back to see Bert,' said Mum, when she came in to see them after the visitor had gone.

'It was very kind of her coming all that way really. I'm sorry you don't like her. She's not a very happy person, you know.'

'I'd be happy with all those rabbits. I'd be happy with just one rabbit,' said Debbie.

'Yes, love. Time for bed now.'

Mum came up to check that they'd washed properly.

'Somebody wiped dirt on their towel yesterday,' she said, 'and their flannel wasn't even wet.'

She made David get out of bed again to wash behind his knees.

'Sleep tight,' she said. 'See you in the morning. Dad and I do love you, you know.'

David sat up in bed again after Mum had gone downstairs. He wanted to finish reading the comic Dad had given him that morning. He'd only two more pages to go.

It didn't take long, and as he put it back on the little table by his bed he noticed his Bible. Mum must have put it there when she unpacked for him. He picked it up and opened it, and then he put it back where he'd found it. God was his friend of course, but it did seem that he'd let David down.

'It wouldn't do any harm to talk to him though, I suppose,' thought David.

'Hello, God,' he said. 'I expect you know I've been in trouble. I did tell you I wanted Dad back, and when you didn't do anything, I went to get him, but that didn't do any good either. I hope,' went on David, 'that you have better luck with other people's prayers. I still want to be your friend though,' David finished off, 'because Mr. Shaw says you're the best one he's got, and I believe him. Goodbye from David Holmes.'

David remembered what Mr. Shaw had said once about thanking God, too.

'Before you go,' said David, 'I'd like to say thank you for my sisters and for my Mum and Dad loving me. Goodbye again.'

David could hear Mum putting the milk bottles out and bolting the door. He wondered what she'd told the man in the shoe shop about missing work that morning. Still, he didn't really care, he was glad to be home.

The next morning there was a letter when he got down to breakfast. There was one each for Alison and Debbie too. They were all from Dad.

'I like getting letters,' said Debbie. 'I hope he writes every week.'

'He might if you write back,' said Mum.

In David's letter Dad wrote about what he'd done at work, and said he hoped to take them out to the Safari Park on Saturday. David told Mum.

'That's tomorrow,' she said. 'Something to look forward to.'

'Hope it doesn't rain again,' said Debbie.

'And we hope you're not sick,' said Alison.

'Oh you,' said Debbie, 'just because I'm youngest.'

'It's time for school,' said Mrs. Holmes pushing back her chair. 'Good job you don't have letters every day.'

Chapter Eleven

David wrote all about his outing in his news book on the following Monday.

'I want you to try to make your news sound a bit more interesting,' said Miss Lawson.

'That'll be easy today,' thought David.

He started on a clean page, ruled a margin and put the date.

'On Saturday,' he began, 'I went to the Safari Park with my Dad and two sisters. It cost £1 to get in. It was good there. Some munkies climed on the car and we made faces at them. The loins were good, then we got out of the car and lookt round, there were some good animals. We went to the dolfinairium and watched the show. My sister got splashed. On the way home Debbie fell asleep and I banged my hed on the window.'

He showed it to Miss Lawson,

'You're lucky,' she said. 'Didn't you go to the zoo last week?'

'No, the week before,' said David. 'Our Dad takes us out every Saturday now, and sometimes on Sunday.'

'Just write out your spelling mistakes three times,' said Miss Lawson, 'then you can do your Maths.'

David went back to the table he was sharing with Gary. Gary hadn't managed to write very much, he found it very difficult. So David told him how to spell some words.

He felt sorry for Gary. His mum and dad never

took him out. He had to play in the street all the time too, because his mum didn't like him in the house.

'You coming up the rec. tonight?' asked Gary.

'No,' said David, 'I've got to go to Cubs.'

'Is it good?' asked Gary.

'Yes, you ought to join. It doesn't cost much.'

Then Miss Lawson called over,

'Come on, you two,' she said, 'stop gossiping and get on with your work please.'

David stayed behind again after Cubs. He wanted to have a word with Mr. Shaw.

'Sorry I haven't been to Sunday Club for a couple of weeks,' said David, 'but we've had to go out.'

'That's all right, David, You know you're more than welcome any time.'

Mr. Shaw put some balls and ropes back in the Cub box.

'How are you getting on with praying now?'

'I'm not. I think I'll give it up. It doesn't seem to work for me.'

'That's a shame. What seems to be the problem?'

'Well there were two things I told you about. I asked God and he just didn't do anything. I talked to him like you said and I even thanked him for some things, but it didn't make any difference.'

'It dces seem hard, doesn't it? But it wouldn't be God's way to force your dad to do something. He's not like that. He lets people choose for themselves. Now that your dad's decided that he'll live away from you all, God will let him go ahead. I know that upsets you, but I'm sure your dad and God still love you.'

'Mum said she would be upset if Dad came back. So – so no one's going to be happy either way, are they?'

'I suppose not. I'll tell you something, David. I don't expect God to solve all my problems, or wave a magic wand and make everything right, but I do expect him to help me to get along and make the best of it.'

'Doesn't God ever give people nice things then?'

'Oh yes, of course, but not always when you're expecting it. It comes as a surprise then.'

'Oh.'

'You think about it. Come and talk again if you want to.'

'All right. Thanks very much.'

David went outside. He hadn't got his bike with him. It had a puncture. Mum had given him some money for chips, and when he arrived at the shop he found some of the boys there ahead of him.

'We've got to wait a few minutes,' said Stephen. 'The man's just put a new batch in the fat.'

'What did you all do tonight then?' said Mr. Hopkins, the fish and chip man. 'I could hear you right up the street.'

'That was probably British Bulldog,' said David. 'It does get a bit rough sometimes.'

'Well, blow me. I thought you boys spent your time working and taking tests, not playing games.'

'We do that first,' said Stephen. 'The games bit is at the end.'

'Oh, I see,' said Mr. Hopkins. 'I think the chips are done now.'

They all went outside with their chips, and sat on the wall of the house next door to eat them. They were very hot when you bit them, especially the big ones.

'Wish we had chips more often at school,' said Stephen, 'instead of that horrid mashed stuff. I hate it.'

'Wonder if they have chips in Wales,' said David.

'They do,' mumbled Michael with a chip in his mouth. 'My brother went last year.'

'I'm going next year,' said Stephen, 'my Mum said I could.'

David didn't say anything. When they'd finished their chips, they put the papers in the box Mr. Banks left outside for them and walked up the road.

David was meant to go straight home after Cubs and what with the chips and talking to Mr. Shaw it was getting quite late. So when they reached the entrance to his back alley, he said goodnight and hurried down it.

He played the dog game as he went. It was one he'd made up a month or so ago, and so far the dog had won every time. The game was to get past number seven's garden without the dog barking.

This time he crouched down so that the dog couldn't see him over the fence, and crept very slowly forward. He didn't make one single little noise, but just as he got to the bottom of number seven the dog began to growl.

'Bother,' said David, and stood up.

Then the dog bounded down the garden and leapt up on the fence with its front paws resting on the top. It was barking and growling and looked very vicious.

David stuck his tongue out at it and walked on. He liked dogs, but not that one.

'That dog's having a go tonight,' said Mum as David walked into the kitchen. 'I hope you haven't been teasing it.'

'No,' said David, 'but don't be surprised if it gets me one of these days.'

'Don't talk daft,' said Mrs. Holmes, 'that dog's very well trained.'

'That's what I mean, Mum. Number Seven don't like children.'

'And nor would I,' said Mrs. Holmes, 'if balls kept coming in my garden catching me on the head.'

'It was an accident. Can I have some milk please?'

'Yes, it's in the fridge.'

Mum was doing the ironing.

'Was Cubs good?' she said.

'Yes, not bad. Are there any chocolate cakes left?'

'Afraid not, Alison had the last one not ten minutes ago. There are some chocolate biscuits in the tin, though. A new sort. I only bought them today.'

'I'll try those.'

'Chris and Geoffrey are in Wales now, aren't they?'

'Yes.'

'Did you mind very much about not going?'

'I did at first.'

'Well, love, we'll try and get you there next year, and that's a promise.'

'Oh thanks, Mum. Stephen's going then.'

'Who's he, dear? I don't think you've talked about him.'

'He goes to Cubs. He's a new boy this term.'

'Oh I see. By the way, David, there's a surprise for you in the front room. I know how upset you've been about dad and your Wales trip. I wanted to make it up to you a bit. It's not much but. . . .'

'Can I go and see, Mum?'

'Yes, of course.'

David rushed along the passage, and into the front room. Whatever it was, was huge. All the space in front of the fireplace was taken up by an enormous brown box. David had no idea what it could be. He stood for a few moments just looking, and then very carefully he bent down and undid the box at one end. It was still almost impossible to tell what was inside, except that it was made of green metal. So he tugged, and pulled, and fought a battle with the box, until at last it tore and the contents shot out on to the carpet.

Then, of course, he couldn't really believe that what he was seeing was really there. He just couldn't believe it belonged to him. It was an enormous table football game, something he'd never dreamed of having.

'Well, do you like it, son?' asked Mum. She was standing in the doorway.

'It's just fantastic, Mum. It really is.'

'Come on then,' said Mum, 'Let's put it together.' She bent down and started screwing on the legs.

When it was assembled, they called the girls in and had a game. It was a bit hectic and Mum said she thought it would probably take a bit of practice before they were any good at it.

Later on, when he was in bed, Alison came in and told him how she'd helped Mum to choose it from Auntie Betty's catalogue. She said that Mum would have to pay back 50p a week for ages.

But David was so happy and so pleased that Mum had thought of him especially, that he didn't worry about the money at all.

He had meant to talk to God when he went to bed. But he was so tired that he fell asleep almost at once. But he remembered in the morning and had a few words before he went down to breakfast.

'Morning, God,' he started. 'I'm glad you're still my friend and that you'll always be here; and thank you for everything.' That sounded a bit vague, so David said, 'Thank you for my bike, and for Mum saying I can go to Wales next year. It's only school today, but please help me to make the best of it. Mum and Dad are going to work, perhaps you could keep an eye out for them too. Thank you very much from David Holmes.'

'Come on, David,' called Mum up the stairs, 'I won't call you again.'

'Coming,' he shouted, and picked up his sweater and training shoes before leaping downstairs.

Mum had his bacon and fried bread ready in his place. The girls were half way through theirs.

'Now don't shovel it down, David,' said Mum. 'You'll get indigestion. I'm taking Deb to the dentist after school today, so you'll have to let yourselves in. The key is under the dustbin.'

'All right, Mum.'

David walked to school with Debbie. She was helping him to carry some old cardboard boxes he wanted for a model.

'Do you like the dentist?' she asked.

'Not much.'

'I hate it. It frightens me.'

'There's no need.'

'That's what Mum says, but she won't come in with me like she used to.'

'Well you're older now. The dentist would think you were daft. God's with you anyway.'

'Is he really?'

'Of course. He's everywhere. I'll have a word with him about it, or you could if you liked. He can't stop it hurting, but at least you're not alone.

'That's the thing about God, Debbie. He doesn't make everything fun and easy, but he helps you not to feel too bad.'

Just then Debbie dropped all the boxes and they had to stop and sort them out again.

'Don't get them bashed up,' warned David. 'I'm going to make a space capsule with them.'

In the playground David made Debbie give the boxes to Gary.

'Don't worry about the dentist,' he said. 'I'll see you later.'

Then he and Gary talked about the space capsule and how they were going to make it, until the whistle went. While they were waiting for Miss Lawson to take the register, David spoke to God in his head.

'Just a quick talk to let you know that Debbie's going to the dentist. She might contact you herself, but if not please look after her. Bye for now from David.'

David looked round and smiled at Gary.

'It's a good thing we've got friends,' he thought as he gave Gary a jab with his pencil.

Chapter Twelve

It was hot the next afternoon. David could smell the tar melting on the road, and the petrol fumes from passing cars as he walked slowly home from school.

He had a stick in his hand which he'd found in the school playground. It was all twisted and gnarled. As he ambled past the rec. he ran it along the iron railings. It made his hand vibrate.

When he came to the end of the railings, he looked up. He could just see his house on the other side of the road. The windows were catching the sun, like mirrors.

David waited for a break in the traffic and crossed over. Now he had an uninterrupted view right down the road to where he lived. It was a long way, but he could see a girl playing outside on the wall. He thought it was probably Debbie.

As he came closer, he could see that she had something furry in her arms. It was next door's kitten.

'You're home early, Deb,' he said, slinging his football bag on to the front step. Then he bent down and tickled the kitten behind its ears. It wriggled a bit, then purred even louder.

'Oh no,' said Debbie. 'Look what's coming.'

It was the alsatian from number seven. On a lead, of course, with Mrs. Jakes on the other end.

Debbie cuddled the kitten closer to her chest as the dog padded nearer. The kitten didn't seem very frightened, but just as it drew level, the alsatian let out a low growl. Then it all started to happen.

David saw the kitten tense up, before taking an enormous leap from Debbie's arms on to the pavement. Then it was off, up the road with Debbie racing after it. It moved incredibly fast, its paws hardly touching the ground, while Debbie trundled along, arms swinging and breath coming fast.

David joined in the chase too. He was sure he'd get there first. The kitten was way ahead though, darting about a bit, but keeping a good lead. The dog all forgotten, David and Debbie could think only of catching the creature.

David could feel the sweat in his hair, his chest felt tight. He couldn't go on much longer, and he hadn't even caught up with Debbie. Then, just as he thought the chase would never end, the kitten swerved between the parked cars and on to the road. Debbie followed, hurtling herself round off the edge of the kerb.

David felt horror seize him in the stomach. As if it was a slow motion film he could see the kitten, and Debbie and a car speeding down the road towards her.

He rushed forwards, his heart pounding, his mouth gone dry. Time seemed endless. Those few steps between him and the girl went on for ever.

Almost there, he threw himself at her. His outstretched hands grabbed her ankles and pulled her back into the gap made by the parked cars. She fell forwards, banging her head on the road. At the same time the car screeched to a halt. The car door banged and a man stood over them. He was white and his hands shook.

'Lucky escape for you, young lady,' he said. 'Good job you were there, son.'

He helped them up. Then he fetched the kitten and handed it to David. Both the children had bleeding knees and Debbie had a scraped forehead too.

'Are you all right? Can I take you home?' asked the man.

'No thanks,' said David. 'We only live down the road.'

Debbie was sobbing, and David put his arm round her. He took her slowly home.

'Where's the kitten?' Debbie managed to stammer.

'He's safe,' said David. 'I've got him. It's all right.' David couldn't think straight as he walked Debbie home. The sound of the car's brakes screeching kept echoing in his ears. He felt very sick.

They let themselves into the house. Mum had gone shopping. So David bathed Debbie's knees and face, and put some plasters on for her. She stopped crying, but she was still very shaky.

'I would have been hit,' she said. 'I was nearly hit. I'm frightened.'

'It's all over now,' said David. 'All over. Try and forget about it.'

He gave her a glass of milk and a biscuit, and made her blow her nose. Then suddenly he knew. It was as if he'd always known it really, but had forgotten or just not understood. He knew that God cared.

If he had gone to Wales on the school trip, he wouldn't have been playing with the kitten on a hot summer afternoon, and Debbie might have run out on the road and been killed. She'd needed him, and he, David Holmes, had been important.

'Come on, Debbie,' he said. 'Let's go outside and sit in the front again. We won't tell Mum what really happened. Let's just say we fell over.'

David walked down the hall towards the open front door. He felt very happy and, as he came out into the sunlight, he smiled.